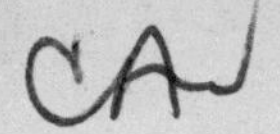

"Looks like you're not going to cut me any slack, are you?"

"Why should I?" Angie quickly countered.

"All right, I deserve that. But when I saw you, I was shocked. What are you doing here on the Sandbur?"

"I'm working. What are you doing? Rubbing elbows with the rich? Oh, sorry. I forgot—you *are* the rich."

Frowning, Jubal stepped closer. "You're still a very beautiful girl, Angie, but you've changed. That's easy to see."

"I'm not a girl anymore, I'm a woman. And no, I haven't changed. When we were together you just never saw this side of me."

When she'd been dating Jubal she'd been a loving, carefree person. There hadn't been a bitter bone in her body—*until he'd decided to marry someone else.*

Dear Reader,

Here in the warm climate of South Texas, Christmas is my very favorite time of the year. Palms, banana trees and even shrimp boats are strung with colorful lights, and in family yards nativity scenes reveal the true meaning of the season.

On the Sandbur Ranch, Angela Malone is helping everyone get ready for Christmas, except herself. As a single mother, her holidays are lean and lonely. This year all she's hoping for is to give her daughter Melanie a few of the gifts on her list—anything more would be a miracle.

But Christmas is also a time for surprises, and Angela gets a huge one when she comes face-to-face again with her daughter's father, a man who walked out of her life five years ago. Is she finally going to get the Christmas she always wanted?

I hope you enjoy reading how Jubal shows Angie that love, family and togetherness is what Christmas is all about!

Merry Christmas and God bless each trail you ride!

Stella Bagwell

THE CHRISTMAS SHE ALWAYS WANTED

STELLA BAGWELL

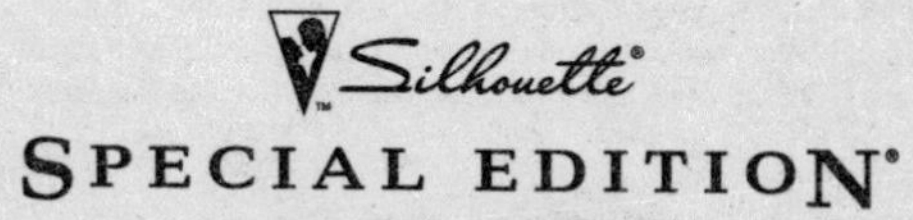

Published by Silhouette Books
America's Publisher of Contemporary Romance

ISBN-13: 978-0-373-24935-0
ISBN-10: 0-373-24935-7

THE CHRISTMAS SHE ALWAYS WANTED

This edition published by arrangement with Harlequin Books S.A.

Visit Silhouette Books at www.eHarlequin.com

Printed in U.S.A.

Books by Stella Bagwell

Silhouette Special Edition

Found: One Runaway Bride #1049
**Penny Parker's Pregnant!* #1258
White Dove's Promise #1478
†*Should Have Been Her Child* #1570
†*His Defender* #1582
†*Her Texas Ranger* #1622
†*A Baby on the Ranch* #1648
In a Texas Minute #1677
†*Redwing's Lady* #1695
†*From Here to Texas* #1700
†*Taming a Dark Horse* #1709
†*A South Texas Christmas* #1789
†*The Rancher's Request* #1802
†*The Best Catch in Texas* #1814
†*Having the Cowboy's Baby* #1828
Paging Dr. Right #1843
†*Her Texas Lawman* #1911
†*Hitched to the Horseman* #1923
†*The Christmas She Always Wanted* #1935

*Twins on the Doorstep
†Men of the West

Silhouette Books

The Fortunes of Texas
The Heiress and the Sheriff

Maitland Maternity
Just for Christmas

A Bouquet of Babies
*"Baby on Her Doorstep"

Midnight Clear
*"Twins under the Tree"

Going to the Chapel
"The Bride's Big Adventure"

STELLA BAGWELL

began writing romance novels more than twenty years ago. Now, more than sixty books later, she likens her job to childbirth. The pain is great, but the rewards are too sweet to measure.

Stella married her high school sweetheart thirty-seven years ago and now the two live on the Texas coast where the climate is tropical and the lifestyle blessedly slow. When Stella isn't spinning out tales of love, she's usually working outdoors on their little ranch, 6 Pines, helping her husband care for a herd of very spoiled horses.

They have a son, Jason, who is a high school math teacher and athletic coach.

To my son, Jason,
for keeping all my technical gadgets going!

Love you!

Chapter One

"How do I look? Fine enough to serve dinner guests?"

Lifting her arms away from her body, Angela Malone turned on the heel of her sandal in front of the Sandbur cook, then dropped a playful curtsy.

"Hmm," Cook said, as she thoughtfully surveyed her young helper. "If you took off the apron you'd look like a princess in that little black dress. But since we're serving barbecue tonight, you might ought to keep it on."

Angela was inclined to agree. The little black dress was just a simple cotton sheath, but in spite of her having worked as a waitress at The Cattle Call Café for the past two years, she wasn't always the most graceful. There had been times gravy and sauces had landed on her instead of on the table she was serving. But that was then. She'd moved up in life since her friend Nicci Saddler Garroway had gotten her this job on the Sandbur Ranch in south

Texas. Now she was Cook's kitchen assistant in the "big house" where the matriarch Geraldine Saddler and her son, Lex, resided. Besides helping Cook prepare and serve meals, Angela also oversaw the maids' housecleaning, shopped for both households and generally took care of any leftover task that the maids couldn't deal with.

"You're probably right about the apron, Cook," Angela told the woman. "But I do want Ms. Saddler to think I look presentable. She really seems to want to put on the dog tonight."

Cook, a tall, thin woman in her seventies with hair that was more black than gray and lips painted as deep a red as her fingernails, walked over to where Angela was about to pick up a tray of appetizers.

"Don't be nervous, honey. You've served many a table before." Reaching up, she adjusted the tortoise-shell barrette that was holding the front of Angela's heavy, brown hair off her face, then patted her cheek. "Pretty as a June mornin'. Now shoo. Go on with those appetizers before Geraldine comes back here to see why we're dawdlin'."

Grinning, Angela picked up the tray. "I'm on my way!"

Shouldering her way through the kitchen's swinging door, Angela hurried down the long hallway that would lead her to the formal living room. Along the way, the smell of smoked shrimp, brought fresh from San Antonio Bay only the previous day, wafted up to her nose, reminding her that she'd not taken time to eat since breakfast at five that morning.

With a dinner party scheduled, she'd not had time to do anything, except help Cook prepare a whole table of elaborate dishes and make sure the maids had cleaned all the rooms and arranged fresh flowers.

As Angela neared the opening of the living room, she caught the sound of voices, both male and female, intermixed with light laughter. In the background, a CD of Bob Wills and his Texas Playboys was softly playing a waltz.

One, two, three. One, two, three, she silently hummed to the beat. How lovely it would be to be dancing, waltzing in the arms of some nice guy who didn't care that she was a single mother.

Pushing that wishful thought away, Angela took a deep breath and stepped into the living room. One quick glance from the corner of her eye told her the space was full of people.

Careful to skirt the crowd, many of whom were standing about the room in small groups, Angela headed straight to a long table that had been set up near the wet bar. She was about to place the tray of shrimp next to a platter of fried jalapeños when Geraldine Saddler spoke up from behind her.

"Angie, if that's the shrimp, bring it over here, please. There's plenty of space on the coffee table."

Turning quickly to follow the woman's orders, Angela made her way to the middle of the room where a chesterfield couch and matching armchairs were grouped around a low coffee table.

As she carefully placed the tray on the polished oak, Geraldine spoke behind her.

"You should try these, Jubal. They'll melt in your mouth."

Angela momentarily froze. Surely it wasn't *him!* He couldn't be the new veterinarian for the Sandbur, the reason for this party, she thought wildly.

Her heart thudding with heavy dread, she slowly raised her head and found herself staring into the face that she'd spent the past five years desperately trying to forget.

Jubal. She didn't know whether she whispered the name, mouthed it with her lips or silently shouted it. In any case, she could feel the blood draining from her face, hear a loud rushing noise in her ears.

She watched a flicker of recognition, then shock, cross his face, but she didn't wait around to see if he would actually acknowledge her. She excused herself to Geraldine, then practically raced from the room.

By the time she got back to the kitchen, she was out of breath and her legs were so weak that all she could do was slump onto a bench seat.

Seeing Angela's shaky entrance, Cook dropped a pair of tongs and hurried over to her. "Angie, what's wrong, girl? You look like you're gonna be sick!"

Gulping in breaths of air, Angela wiped at the sweat that had popped out suddenly on her brow and upper lip. "I—I'm okay, Cook. I think—I've gone too long without eating."

That was true enough, Angela thought, as Cook stood with her hands on her hips, her black eyes full of concern.

"Hmmp. Well, it's funny to me that you just now remembered you were starving." Her red lips puckered into a frown. "What happened in there?"

There was no need for Cook to explain that "in there" meant the living room where *he* had been sitting with the Sandbur families and their friends.

"Nothing."

"Did you spill the tray? Trip over somebody?"

She'd tripped all right, and fallen. But that had happened five years ago, she thought miserably.

"Everything is—okay, Cook. I just feel shaky."

Closing her eyes, Angela tried to tamp down the panic racing through her. How could she go back in there and serve five courses around a table where he'd be sitting, she wondered frantically.

"Here. Eat some of this while I get the salads ready," Cook ordered. "Maybe that'll put some color in your cheeks."

Angela opened her eyes to see the old woman placing a small plate filled with Texas caviar and several saltine crackers in front of her. Her throat was so tight, she wasn't sure she could swallow anything, but she forced herself to shovel up some of the mixture of black-eyed peas, onions and peppers on one of the crackers and pop it into her mouth.

After a few more bites of the spicy vegetables, Angela rose to her feet and joined Cook at the long counter. The woman needed her, and now was hardly the time for Angela to allow her emotions to immobilize her. "I'll finish this," she assured the woman. "You go ahead with whatever you need to be doing."

Cook frowned as she glanced at Angela's still-pale face. "You look like you've fallen in a flour barrel. Maybe I'd better call Miss Nicci back here to check on you. Even young people have heart attacks."

Her heart was full of pain, all right. But not the sort that Cook was worried about. "You're not about to bother Nicci this evening! Her off-duty time is always being interrupted with medical emergencies. I'm not going to ruin this dinner party for her."

"Angie—"

Before Cook could protest, Angela placed a reassuring hand on her arm. "Cook, don't worry about me. I—I don't have anything medically wrong with me." Deciding it would be easier to confide in Cook than to hide the truth, she added, "I just—saw someone at the party. Someone I haven't seen in a long time. And I—well, I never expected to see him again. Ever. It was shocking to me. That's all."

Instead of plying her with personal questions, Cook tactfully asked, "You want me to call Alida over to take your place tonight?"

Alida was one of the maids that had worked for the Saddler and Sanchez families for several years. At the moment she was at Angela's house, babysitting Angela's daughter, Melanie, and as far as Angela was concerned, that was where she was going to stay.

Straightening her shoulders, Angela set her jaw with determination. "No. I'll be fine. Just fine."

Out in the living room, Jubal Jamison struggled to focus on the conversation going on around him. Seeing Angie again had shaken the very earth beneath him. Dear God, he'd never expected to see her beautiful face again. Not after she'd left Cuero five years ago. What was she doing here? Obviously she was employed by the ranch, although no one had bothered to tell him. But then why would they, he thought grimly. No one on the Sandbur knew that Angela had once been the love of his life.

So what are you going to do now, big boy? Run? Turn away from her again?

Not this time, Jubal silently swore. After she'd left town, he believed he'd never be given the chance to see Angie again. He wasn't about to pass up this opportunity to connect with her once more. Besides, he'd already moved onto the Sandbur. An animal clinic was currently being constructed smack in the middle of the ranch yard. Costly high-tech equipment, being shipped from Dallas, was scheduled to arrive any day.

Someone announced that dinner was ready and like a zombie Jubal shuffled along to the dining room with the rest of the guests. Moments later he found himself seated to the right of Geraldine Saddler at the head of the dinner table.

The room was long, the ceiling low and crossed with rough-hewn beams of cypress wood. Along one wall, a row of arched windows displayed a view of the backyard where the trunks of Mexican palms were decorated with tiny, clear lights, signifying the coming holidays. Back at the long table, fresh gold and red flowers were arranged at intervals down the center, adding even more vivid color to the scene.

Jubal had grown up in an affluent home, but he had to admit his parents' social events were modest compared to this Sandbur affair. Even so, Geraldine and her family were very down-home, laid-back people. Too bad his parents couldn't have been more like them. Maybe then they could have understood his relationship with Angie. But then, his parents weren't responsible for their separation. Unfortunately, he'd been the guilty party. And he'd been paying the price ever since.

By the time Angela had served after-dinner coffee, she'd worked herself up to a numb fury. Throughout the meal, Jubal had ignored her. He'd not even had the decency to give her a simple hello. It wasn't like that icky wife of his had been sitting by his side, watching his every move. A polite greeting from him was all she'd expected. But he'd not even been enough of a gentleman to give her that much.

"Damn the man," she muttered under her breath as she stomped back to the kitchen.

"They're digging into dessert right now," Angela said to Cook, who was sitting at a long, pine table, her thin, bony hands wrapped around a coffee cup. In her early seventies, the woman should have looked exhausted. Instead, she looked contented.

"There'll be some more visiting done before the guests leave, but you don't need to wait around. Go on home to your little girl. I'll see that the maids get everything cleared away."

Frowning, Angela eased onto the bench seat directly across from Cook. "I'm not about to leave this mess with you. And why are you looking so happy? Aren't you tired?"

The woman chuckled. "'Course I'm tired. But it always makes me happy to put out a good feed for Geraldine's friends. Those fancy cooks on TV couldn't have done it better."

"You're proud of your job," Angela said, then added wistfully, "I wish—"

When she stopped abruptly, Cook prompted, "What, child, what do you wish?"

Angela sighed. "I wish that my mother could have been more like you, Cook. In the little town where I used to live, Mom worked as a cook in a restaurant. She always griped about the job and said that cooking was poor folks' work. But nothing much made her happy anyway."

"Humph," Cook snorted. "She must have needed some head doctoring. I feel just as good as anybody out there." She inclined her dark head in the direction of the living room where the party was still going strong.

"So do I," Angela agreed. As for Nadine Malone, Angela didn't know whether her mother was still cooking in the Mustang Café or if her parents even still lived on their farm near Cuero. She'd not seen them since they'd labeled her as worthless and kicked her out of the family home.

Sighing, Angela rose to her feet and walked over to the row of cluttered cabinets. Seeing Jubal tonight was bad enough without her dwelling on her parents, who'd turned their backs on their daughter at the time when she'd needed them the most.

A half hour later, the two women had the kitchen organized enough to call it a night. Angela exited the back of the house carrying a box full of leftovers, enough for two or three suppers for her and Melanie.

In the backyard, she walked along a path lit with footlights until she reached the far western side of the house where she'd parked her little economy car beneath a live-oak. She was carefully placing the box of food on the back floorboard when she heard the faint crunch of gravel directly behind her.

Glancing over her shoulder, she saw Jubal. Alone. And walking directly toward her.

Hating the way her heart was pounding, Angela shut the door, then turned to face him. The man had hurt her in ways she didn't want to think about. All she should be feeling at this moment was intense hatred. But try as she might, she couldn't hate him. After all, he'd given her the most precious gift a man could give a woman. His child.

"Hello, Angie."

There was only a small filtering of light slanting from the big house to the spot where they were standing. She could barely make out his face, but that didn't matter. She'd not forgotten the shape of his rough, hawkish features, the gold flecks in his green eyes, the thick tumble of sandy-brown hair falling across a wide forehead. His face was too striking to ever forget.

She swallowed. "Hello, Jubal."

His hands were casually stuffed in the pockets of his western-cut trousers and, as her eyes flicked up and down the long length of him, she realized his body had remained fit the past five years. His shoulders were still broad, his thighs muscular, his waist just as trim as the day she'd first seen him, squatted on his heels, doctoring her father's sick goat.

After a long silence between them, he spoke again, "I've been waiting a few minutes in hopes of catching you. I didn't get a chance to speak to you inside."

Hurt and anger swirled together and simmered in the pit of her stomach. "I served five courses. Guess I wasn't around the table long enough for you to look up and say hello."

He let out a long breath and wiped a hand over his face. She could see his discomfort. See that he didn't know how to deal with her presence. Well, she couldn't feel sorry for the man. He'd made his bed and she hoped he'd been miserable in it.

"Looks like you're not going to cut me any slack, are you?"

"Why should I?" she quickly countered.

He looked toward the big house, then wearily pinched the bridge of his nose. "All right, I deserve that. And I'm sorry I didn't say anything to you sooner." He looked at her. "But seeing you—damn it, I was shocked. What are you doing here on the Sandbur? I never expected to see you in a place like this."

Her nostrils flared as she tried to hold on to her temper. What the hell did he think she was doing? Serving a dinner party just for the fun of it?

"I'm working. What are you doing? Rubbing elbows with the rich?" Instantly, she plopped a hand over her mouth in feigned regret. "Oh, sorry. I forgot—you are the rich."

Frowning, he stepped closer as his gaze swallowed up her pale face. "I expected you to throw some cutting things at me, Angie, but not that."

The last he said with a hint of regret and a glaze of tears was suddenly started burning the back of Angela's eyes. She wasn't a vengeful, vindictive person. So why was she behaving this way to Jubal?

"I'm not a girl anymore, Jubal. I'm a woman. And I guess things—people—look different to me now." Which was true enough, she thought. When she'd been dating Jubal she'd been a happy, loving, carefree person. There hadn't been a bitter bone in her body—until he'd decided to end their relationship and run to another woman. Now she was cautious about putting her trust in anyone.

Drawing his hands out of his pockets, he folded his arms against his chest. Angela's gaze zeroed in on his left hand where it curved around his right elbow. Not for the first time tonight, she noticed his wedding-ring finger was empty. Again, she was reminded that Evette hadn't been by his side tonight. She could only speculate on the woman's whereabouts. This was a big night for Jubal. Angela couldn't imagine the socialite not wanting to share the spotlight with her spouse.

"I had no idea that you were here on the Sandbur," he admitted. "If I'd known—well, I would have looked you up before now."

Five years had passed and she'd not heard a word from him. Until tonight, when happenstance had forced him to see her. She found it difficult to believe that he would have sought her out.

Pain crept through her chest, while sarcasm edged her one word question. "Really?"

From the grimace on his face, he obviously considered her presence on the ranch a nuisance. Well, she could tell him that having him around wasn't exactly making her want to shout hallelujah, either.

"I'm not quite the bastard you think, Angie."

There was no malice or anger in his voice, but then, he had no reason to be spiteful, she thought as she struggled to keep from breaking into sobs. He'd gotten what he wanted.

"I came to work here two months ago," she said hoarsely. "A few days after I'd been on the job, I heard through the grapevine about the ranch hiring a resident vet. I didn't know—until tonight—that it was you. But don't worry, Jubal, I'm not going to give you or your family any problems by trying to stir up old ashes."

He looked uncomfortably down at his boots. "I...wasn't exactly worried about that."

When he didn't add more, Angela decided to plunge ahead. After all, she didn't expect that they would be speaking to each other again. His work here would hardly cause them to brush elbows.

"So—where's Evette? Didn't she want to come to your party tonight?"

His gaze lifted to hers and something in his expression made her heart leap.

"I'm not married to Evette anymore."

Chapter Two

Shock hit Angela's stomach and twisted it into hard knots. "Oh."

"Yeah. Our marriage ended in divorce—about a year after it began."

His features were expressionless as though he were talking about the weather or something mundane, not a life-altering event. As for Angela, emotions were colliding inside her, sending tiny tremors through every nerve in her body. He'd gotten divorced shortly after Melanie had been born. Oh God, if she'd known, what would have happened? Anything?

"Well, I should say I'm sorry. But it's just not in me, Jubal."

His shrug was negligible, as though his divorce meant nothing to him. Angela wanted to scream at him for being so casual. Did he not understand that his marriage had totally devastated her life? Or did he just not care?

"That's all right. Being sorry can't change what happened."

Angela couldn't believe she was standing here with the father of her child, whom she hadn't seen in five long years, discussing his marriage to and divorce from another woman. It was like a ridiculous scene out of a soap opera. And it was angering her like nothing had ever angered her before.

When she finally managed to speak, bitterness coated each word. "You're right. Nothing can change things now."

His features twisted. "Evette was the sort that wouldn't stop until she got what she wanted. And then the game was over."

Is that what Jubal had been to the mayor's daughter? A game? A pawn? The idea made Angela feel even sicker.

"What about your child? Does he or she live with you or Evette?"

Suddenly his face was a mask of cold stone and when he answered, Angela felt as though she'd been punched by a fist.

"She lost the baby midterm. There was a problem with the placenta."

Oh, God. How utterly awful. Not just for Jubal, but for Angela, too. She'd given up this man so that he could marry Evette and be a father to the baby the other woman was carrying. Now he was telling her that the baby hadn't survived.

Angie hadn't believed her heart was capable of breaking any more than it already had, but she'd been wrong. At the moment, it was tearing into tiny, throbbing pieces.

"I don't know what to say, Jubal," she said, her voice hardly above a whisper. "That I'm sorry for you? Sorry for me? Sorry for the whole damn bunch of us? Telling you how I feel right now is…impossible!"

Shaking her head, she turned to her car. "I'd better go," she muttered more to herself than to him.

Jubal couldn't let her go. For the past five years, she'd haunted his days and nights. He'd tried to forget her, tried to tell himself that it was best he let her get on with her life. But that hadn't stopped him from wondering where she'd gone and agonizing over what could have been if things had worked out differently. Tonight when Jubal had looked up and seen her, his heart had somersaulted. Even now, he wanted to touch her, to make sure she was real and not one of his tortured dreams.

"Angie, wait! We haven't—can't we talk a little more?"

"About what?" she asked flatly.

She was even more lovely now, Jubal realized, as his gaze wandered over her. Her heart-shaped face was more lean and angled, her small features more pronounced. He didn't remember her ivory skin being so smooth and pearly, her brown eyes so dark and sultry or her pink lips so full and lush. But then time dimmed everything, he supposed. Except the regret he carried around his heart like a ball and chain. And the passion he still felt for her. As for Angie—she'd loved him deeply once. Were all those feelings truly gone?

He cleared his throat. "Where have you been living all this time?"

Shortly after their relationship had ended, he'd heard that Angela had left town and he'd assumed that she'd moved totally out of the area. How bittersweet to find her so close and yet still so far away.

She glanced over her shoulder at him and he could see from the tight clamp of her lips that she didn't want to talk to him. It crushed him to think that the love she'd once given him was now nothing more than dead ashes buried beneath a heap of anger.

"I've been living in Goliad for the past five years."

She'd been living only thirty minutes away from him! It amazed Jubal that they'd not accidentally crossed paths before now. And if he'd known she was actually that close, would he have gone looking for her? No. He didn't want to think so. He'd made his choice to marry Evette and then struggled to stick with the forced union. Walking away from Angela had been incredibly hard. If he'd seen her in that awful year when he was trying to make things work with Evette, he might not have had the strength to walk away again. And after their marriage had ended, he'd felt like a complete loser. He'd convinced himself that Angie was much better off without him and the baggage of horrible mistakes he carried around with him.

"Oh," he said. "Guess you've had time to get to know a lot of people around here."

"A few. The Saddlers and Sanchezes are some of the best."

In spite of her work clothes and weary face, she looked utterly beautiful and Jubal felt himself moving forward, closer to the woman who'd irrevocably changed his life.

"I guess I'm trying to ask if you're married now?"

For a split second he saw a spark in her eyes as though she wanted to jump straight at him with claws bared, but then just as quickly her face went eerily placid and she quickly glanced away from him.

"No," she said bluntly. "I'm still single. Not that it's any of your business. And right now I really do have to get home."

By the time she'd opened the driver's door, Jubal was at her side, his hand curling around her arm. The moment he touched her, she jerked as though he'd shot her with a bullet. As for Jubal, he couldn't remember a time he'd felt so completely shaken, so aware of another human being in his life. She was single! The news shouldn't mean anything to him. But hope was surging through him like a ray of sunshine amidst thunderclouds, and he wanted to cling to it. The same way he wanted to cling to her.

"Angie," he said in a low, raspy voice, "I'm sorry about tonight. Sorry about all the pain and mess I put you through with Evette."

She closed her eyes, as though to shut him out of her sight. All Jubal wanted to do was pull her into his arms.

"I don't want to hear it, Jubal. Your apologies are too little, too late."

Jubal felt sick inside. She'd once trusted him completely. She'd once looked up to him, respected him. Loved him. Oh, how he wanted that Angie again. Would he ever see that loving woman again?

Biting back a sigh, he tried to be diplomatic. "Look Angie, with both of us working here, don't you think we should try to be civil to each other?"

Her eyes fluttered open and her cold stare bored straight into him. "The Sandbur is a huge ranch. It's not likely we'll be running into each other that much."

In other words, she didn't want to have anything to do with him. But then, what did he expect? He'd hurt her badly. He didn't deserve her civility or respect. But he wanted it. And wanted her.

"Not likely, but possible," he said. "A few days ago, I moved into the house below the north hill."

A lifeless smile tilted her lips. "Good for you. I live here on the ranch, too. In the house where Darla Ketchum and her daughter Raine used to live. So now we both know the spots to avoid. And as far as I'm concerned, I'd be a happy woman if I never saw you again. So stay away from me! Got it?"

Her cutting words were bad enough, but it was the callous sarcasm with which she spoke them that shoved Jubal in the wrong direction. He probably did deserve her scorn, but he hated to hear that coldness in her voice. He wanted to bring her back to life, to spark in her the same desire that had been burgeoning inside him from the first moment he'd spotted her tonight in the Saddler living room.

Before he could consider his actions, his hand tightened on her arm and tugged her against him.

"Okay, Angie, you've shown me how you feel," he muttered. "Now I think it's about time I gave you a clue to how I feel."

Her eyes flew wide open as her hands pressed uselessly against his chest. "Jubal—"

Blindly, his lips swooped down on hers, snatching them up in a kiss that was full of frustration, loss and longing. She tasted exactly the way he remembered: sweet, exotic, precious. Five years ago, he'd not been able to get enough of her and apparently that hadn't changed. His body was already reacting, burning to make love to her again.

A few yards away in the dark shadows, a dog barked, and even farther, a truck engine roared to life. The distractions splintered Jubal's foggy senses and forced him to finally rip his mouth away from hers.

Stunned, Angela stared at him, trying to read something on his face that would explain the kiss. But his expression was mostly shuttered and she felt herself floundering, too shaken to speak or gather the shreds of her composure.

"Angie, I—" He paused long enough to draw in a ragged breath. "Apologizing is about all I seem to be doing tonight, isn't it?"

No. He'd done far more, she thought bitterly. He'd turned her world upside down. Again. He'd put his mouth on hers and that's all it had taken to prove that she hadn't gotten this man out of her system.

Her fingers trembling, she raked them through her mussed hair. "I don't know what you're thinking, Jubal, but I'm not your girl anymore. And you don't have the right to kiss me—to even speak to me," she finished in a raw whisper.

"Hell, Angie, being near you—makes me forget about the time we've been apart. Tonight, I feel like I'm seeing you for the first time all over again."

Feeling as though she was splintering into a thousand pieces, she jerked her arm away from his grasp. "Well, get over it, Doc. Because nothing will make me forget what you've done to me!"

Not waiting for a reply, Angela climbed into her car and slammed the door. Without even glancing his way, she started the engine and gunned the car backwards. From the corner of her eye, she could see Jubal quickly stepping aside, out of the car's path. After that, a wall of tears blurred her vision and she could barely see to drive home.

The next morning, as Angela helped her four-and-a-half-year-old daughter dress, she tried to hide her exhaustion and put on a cheery face while she listened to Melanie's chatter.

"Mommy, I'm really, really hungry this mornin'. Can I have bacon, please?"

"Hmm. I suppose so. But you have to eat your oatmeal, too."

Melanie clapped her little hands together. "Yippee. Thank you! And can I have some of those meat things? That look like sticks?"

"Those are sausage links," Angela said as she held out a pair of blue jeans for Melanie to step into. "And we don't have any of those right now. I'll get you some when I go to the grocery store."

Angela adjusted the waistband at Melanie's rounded waist and reached for a pink sweater with a cartoon character on the front. Since Melanie was not yet old enough for kindergarten and too far away from a preschool, Angela took her to work with her. For the most part she was an obedient child, and both families on the ranch, along with all the employees, were more than happy to help keep an eye on her. Having her child with her was another nice perk of her job and one Angela didn't take lightly.

Back when Angela had been waitressing and struggling to keep a roof over her and Melanie's head, a motherly neighbor, Helga, had often watched Melanie at no charge. Angela always felt guilty, though—afraid she was taking advantage of Helga's generosity. Being here on the Sandbur had taken away many of the difficulties she'd faced with raising Melanie on her own and she'd always be grateful to Nicci for getting her this job.

"Where are we goin' this mornin'? Can we go to Jess's house?"

Jess was the son of Matt and Juliet Sanchez and great-nephew to Geraldine. He was nearing two years old and, at four, Melanie pictured herself as the toddler's mother. When together, the two children had a rip-roaring time. But today she wouldn't be going to the Sanchez house, where the other Sandbur family resided. After last night's party, she needed to make sure the maids were getting the Saddler house back to normal.

"We can't go to Jess's house this morning. We have to help Cook."

Melanie tilted her head from one side to the other and as Angela looked at her precious face, her mind vaulted back to last night. To Jubal and that shattering kiss he'd placed on her lips.

What had he been thinking? Had he believed that she was something he could pick up or lay down anytime he wanted? Or had he really missed her all these years? Could he really still feel something for her?

Don't be stupid, Angela. The man chose to marry another woman instead of you. If he'd ever had feelings for you, he would have shown it then. Not five years later.

Angela was thankful for the voice of reason inside her head, but still it wasn't enough to dim the burst of pure excitement she'd felt when his lips had touched her. For a moment, she'd been transported to a magical place and even this morning when she thought of the kiss, she wanted to close her eyes and sigh.

"Mommy, Mommy! You're not listenin' to me!"

Jerking her attention back to Melanie, Angela saw that her daughter's cherub-like features were scrunched up in a scowl.

"Sorry, honey. Were you saying something?"

"Can I take Mr. Fields with me, pretty please? He can sleep in his basket."

Mr. Fields was an orange tabby that Angela had rescued from the edge of a cotton field where someone had dumped him. At that time, he'd been a scrawny little kitten with a scratched ear and bent tail. Now the tomcat was all grown and patient enough to put up with Melanie's overly zealous affection.

"I suppose so. But he has to stay outside on the patio. And if he gets into a fight with Geraldine's cat then we'll have to bring him home. Okay?"

"Okay! Thank you, Mommy! I'm gonna go get him!"

Before all the words were out of Angela's mouth, the child started to run from the bedroom. Angela jumped to her feet and hurried after her. "Not now, Mel! You have to eat breakfast first." She snatched a hold on Melanie's hand just as the girl was about to twist open the front door. "Come on. You can help me in the kitchen and then we'll get Mr. Fields."

A few minutes later, after a quick breakfast, Angela loaded her daughter and the orange tabby in the car. Since her small house was located on the south edge of the ranch yard, about a mile away from the big Saddler house, it took Angela less than three minutes to make the drive through a maze of barns and corrals, where saddled horses were tied to hitching posts, waiting for cowboys to start their work day.

The first week of December had brought cooler weather to south Texas. Trees were beginning to turn red and yellow. Christmas would be coming soon, and the ranch would be hosting all sorts of parties. Angela would be very busy, but she hardly minded. Her new job would allow her to buy Melanie a few decent gifts this year.

Minutes later, when Angela and Melanie stepped into the kitchen, Cook dropped her scouring pad, then knelt down and opened her arms out to Melanie. The girl ran straight to the older woman and gave her neck a tight hug.

Just to look at the stern woman, Angela wouldn't think

her capable of being soft and affectionate, but she was all that and more with Melanie. Her daughter adored Cook and the feeling was mutual. Early on, Angela had learned from Nicci that Cook had lost her husband at a very young age to the Vietnam war. The couple had not had a chance to have children and afterwards Cook had chosen to live her life alone.

"Well, don't you look pretty this morning with all that brown hair braided." Cook patted the top of Melanie's head where Angela had pinned a coronet of braids. "My husband had brown hair the same color as yours—like an all-day sucker."

Melanie's small nose wrinkled with puzzlement. "What's that?"

Cook chuckled. "A lollipop that tastes like caramel. If your mother can't find you one in the store, I'll make you one. Okay?"

"You wouldn't be spoiling her a bit, now would you, Cook?" Angela asked as she pulled off her lightweight jacket and hung it on a hall tree located in a corner of the kitchen.

"Well, Christmas is coming. It's a time for spoiling." With a final pat to Melanie's cheek, Cook rose and went back to work at the deep, stainless-steel sink.

After Angela settled Melanie with a coloring book at a nearby work table, she joined the other woman. "What do I need to do? Is Miss Geraldine ready for her breakfast yet?"

"No need to worry about that. She's only having toast this morning." She tossed a kitchen towel to Angela. "Here. Dry these pots and then we'll take a coffee break."

"A break! Cook, I didn't take this job to sit around and drink coffee!"

The woman chuckled. "Geraldine don't 'spect you to break your neck from dawn to dusk. Trust me."

Angela decided it was best not to protest. The last person she wanted to irritate was Cook. She'd become like a mother to her and a grandmother to Melanie.

She was drying a second boiling pot, when Cook glanced her way. "Angie, that person last night—the one you got all het up over—is everything okay now?"

The dishtowel paused on the blue granite pot as Angela glanced over at her daughter. Last night after she'd gone to bed, she'd lain awake, reliving Jubal's kiss and wondering how he would react if he learned he had a daughter. With his and Evette's baby dying, would he want to be a part of this child's life? Or would Melanie be an embarrassment to him? The questions had repeatedly tumbled through her mind until she'd fallen asleep from sheer exhaustion. They were still haunting her this morning.

"I'm not sure, Cook."

The older woman tore off a handful of paper towels and began wiping the inside of an iron skillet. "This someone—he wouldn't happen to be the new vet, would he?"

Angela placed the pot and the dishtowel on the cabinet counter and wiped a hand across her forehead. She'd not bothered to put on makeup this morning and she figured she must look pale and exhausted.

"Yes, he would be."

Cook frowned. "That's what I suspected."

Sighing wearily, Angela rested her hip against the cabinets. "We—uh, we knew each other back in Cuero—before he married the mayor's daughter."

Cook's grimace was full of disapproval. "Haven't seen no wife with him around here."

"They're divorced. He told me last night."

"Oh. How you feel about that?"

Picking up the dishtowel, Angela absently twisted it between her hands. "I'm trying not to feel anything toward Jubal Jamison. He's best forgotten."

Cook glanced shrewdly over her shoulder at Melanie, then across to Angela. "Well, if that's what you think."

About six miles north of the main ranch house, Jubal, Matt Sanchez and Lex Saddler were riding across a range filled with three hundred Brahman cows with calves at their sides. The two cousins had invited Jubal to join them on a ride this morning as a way for him to get more familiar with the Sandbur cattle and their quality of grazing.

So far, Jubal had seen healthy cattle and a surprisingly abundant amount of late-season grasses. "These mama cows are in great shape to head into winter," Jubal told the two men. "I don't see that you should change anything about your feeding program."

"Hey, you're my kind of guy, Doc," exclaimed Lex, the younger, blond cousin. "We're gonna be great buddies, I can already tell."

On the other side of Jubal, Matt, the dark, serious one, let out a snorting laugh. "As you can see, Jubal, Lex is always happy when he hears there is less work to do."

Grinning at his cousin's teasing gibe, Lex asked, "Why change something that ain't broke? Right, Doc?"

Jubal chuckled. "Well, there's nothing that I see broken now."

As they rode the horses through the herd of cattle, Jubal visually inspected the animals while the two cousins bantered back and forth. Yet even while he looked for any signs of disease or distress, a part of his mind was replaying the scene he'd had with Angela the night before.

Dear God, seeing her again had dazed him. For the past five years, he'd traveled all over south Texas and had never seen her or even heard anyone mention her. Never would he have dreamed she'd be living here on the Sandbur. And never would he have imagined himself grabbing her like he had and kissing her as though they were still lovers.

Jubal swallowed hard as emotions left the inside of his throat tight. Last night had been too early to tell her about Evette and the baby. But she'd asked and it would've been even worse to avoid the truth. And then he had touched her and every scrap of common sense had left him. Especially when he'd felt her body soften against his, felt her lips begin to respond, the way they'd used to kiss him. Or was that only wishful thinking on his part?

"Hey Jubal, look over there," Matt spoke up. "Something is wrong with that cow's milk bag."

Turning toward Matt, he followed the line of the rancher's pointing finger. "Let's go see. She might need attention."

Moments later, Matt had the cow roped and the lariat secured to his saddle horn. Down on the ground, Jubal stood in knee-high grass as he examined the new mother. "Looks like her teats are inflamed," he told the two men. "She's going to need a shot of medication for the next few days, otherwise her new baby might have to be bottle fed."

"You gonna lead her home, Matt?" Lex asked with a taunting grin. "You've already got her caught."

"Hell, no! She might decide to horn old Ranger. You wanta lead her for five or six miles back to the ranch?" he dared Lex.

For answer, Geraldine's son reached inside his shirt

pocket and pulled out a cell phone. "I'll think I'll just have some of the boys bring out a trailer."

Jubal held up a hand. "Wait. She needs to stay right where she is—with the herd, where she feels safe. It would be best not to put her through the stress of loading her into a stock trailer, then putting her in a dry lot. I'll drive out and take care of her for the next few days."

"I knew there was some good reason we hired you, Doc," Lex said with a happy grin. "I think I just found out what it was."

"Lex, just remember I'm the one who insisted we needed Jubal," Matt told his cousin, then turned a grateful look on Jubal. "I hope you don't regret taking the job."

Regret? The only thing Jubal regretted was losing Angela five years ago. Taking this job had led him back to her. And this time he was going to do things right.

"Not for a minute," Jubal told him.

Chapter Three

Two days later, Angie was back in the kitchen of the big house helping Geraldine wrap dark blue cellophane around two huge baskets.

"Angie, I want you to take these two holiday baskets to Jubal's. Not the clinic, but his house," she said. "They're full of useful little things for his new home and some goodies for him to eat. Men aren't too good about cooking for themselves, you know. You do know how to get there, don't you?"

Angie stared blankly at the woman. She loved her boss and certainly wanted to do everything to please the woman. But go to Jubal's house? The last time she saw him, she'd said that she never wanted to see him again. After that, there was no telling what he'd think when he saw her driving up.

"I—I believe so. It's over the hill, north of the ranch yard. On the left of the road."

"That's right. But the road is too rough for your car. You'd better take my old truck."

The tall, slender, silver-haired woman gathered the cellophane paper at the top of one of the baskets and tied it off with a small piece of grass twine. A masculine touch, for an extremely masculine man, Angela thought wryly.

"Uh—what if he isn't there?" Angela asked.

"Doesn't matter. I seriously doubt he'll have his doors locked. Just take the baskets inside and put the perishables in the refrigerator."

Please, God, don't let him be there, Angela silently prayed. "Yes, ma'am. I'll take care of it right now."

"Take care of what?" Cook asked as she stepped into the kitchen.

Geraldine looked around as Cook approached them. "I'm sending Angie to deliver these baskets to Jubal's house. I want him to feel really at home here on the ranch. Maybe these few things will help."

A tiny frown pulled Cook's brows together as her dark eyes glanced over at Angela. "She don't need to deliver those baskets," she said to Geraldine. "I'll get Alida to do it."

"Alida is over at the Sanchez house," Geraldine reasoned. "And Angela isn't helpless."

Even though she knew the two women had a close relationship that spanned decades, Angela didn't want Cook to get into a rift with Geraldine over her. So when Cook opened her mouth to utter another protest, Angela quickly jumped in. "It's no problem, Cook. I'll get these delivered and be back in no time."

Frowning, Geraldine's glance swung suspiciously back and forth between Angela and Cook. "Is something wrong? Why shouldn't Angela deliver these baskets to Jubal?"

Forcing a cheery smile to her face, Angela swiftly reassured her. "There's nothing wrong, Miss Geraldine. Cook just wants me to help her with a dish we were planning for tonight's meal. That's all."

Seeming to accept Angela's explanation, the ranch lady glanced at the cuffed watch on her wrist. "Well, it's still a long time before supper. You'll have plenty of time to help her."

"Yes, ma'am," Angela replied, then turned and gathered up one of the huge baskets.

"I'll help you carry this one." Cook promptly collected the other basket from the table and followed Angela outside.

At the west side of the house, Angela opened the door to Geraldine's work truck and carefully placed the basket she was carrying on the floorboard. Behind her, Cook snorted.

"Why did you interfere in there, honey? I could've gotten you out of this little job. It's plain to me that you don't want to go to Jubal's house."

"It's all right, Cook. The man probably isn't home anyway."

"Angie, maybe you should fess up to Geraldine," Cook suggested. "Tell her that there's bad blood between you and the doc."

Angela swallowed down a sigh. "There's not bad blood, Cook. Just painful memories. Besides, I can't complain to Miss Geraldine. I'm not important to her and she could easily replace me. Now Jubal—everyone on the ranch already thinks he's just dandy and his job here is very important."

Angela took the basket from Cook's arms and thrust it into the truck.

Scowling, Cook said, "You're important to me. That counts for somethin', don't it?"

Smiling now, Angela turned and kissed the old woman's

cheek. "It counts for everything. Now don't worry about me. I can handle myself around Jubal Jamison."

With that brave statement, she climbed into the truck and headed it toward Jubal's.

As Angela bounced over the rough dirt road washed out from a string of fall rains, she turned up the heater and glanced at the gray sky. Winter in south Texas never lasted long, but it was a dismal time for humans and livestock. This morning Angela was feeling particularly shivery, but she had a feeling the weather had nothing to do with the chill deep inside her.

Facing east, Jubal's cedar-sided house was located on a low, grassy hill with a small creek running in front of it. As she crossed a slab of concrete that spanned the shallow path of water, Angela geared down the truck, then urged the vehicle on up the hill to where a spreading live oak shaded a large, graveled driveway.

She parked the truck, relieved to note that there was no vehicle near the house or the barn. Hopefully, if she worked quickly, she could deposit the baskets inside and be on her way before Jubal showed up.

Pulling the hood of her sweatshirt over her head, she grabbed up one of the baskets and hurried toward the wood-planked porch leading up to the entrance. Along the way, she caught the scent of wood smoke on the wind and looking up spotted a few white puffs coming from the red brick chimney at the right side of the structure.

Stepping up onto the porch, she noticed wicker lawn furniture at one end and a row of potted succulents lined along the wall. Jubal's place looked homey and inviting, a place for a family. But Jubal didn't have a family, she thought with dismay.

The baby Evette had been expecting had never been born. The fact still continued to shock her. Down through the years, she'd imagined Jubal and Evette together, raising their child together, while she and Melanie had struggled by themselves.

Oh God, why couldn't she forget about it? Let it go?

After several knocks on the door, she tried the handle and found it unlocked. Feeling like an interloper, she opened the door wide enough to place the gift basket inside the room, then hurried back to the truck for the second one.

She was in the kitchen, putting the perishable food items in the refrigerator, when she heard the hum of an approaching vehicle minutes later.

Of course it would be Jubal, she thought with sinking dread. At this time of year, no one else would have reason to come back this way.

Bracing herself, she fought the urge to run and waited instead for him to appear. When his tall, lanky body finally stepped through the open doorway of the kitchen, an unexpected thrill rushed through her.

Jubal spotted Angela standing beside the kitchen table and stopped in his tracks. "Oh. It's you," he said with surprise. "I saw Geraldine's truck and thought she was here."

She took an awkward step forward and Jubal could see her cheeks were flushed red, but whether from embarrassment or anger, or simply the cold, he couldn't be sure. In any case, she looked completely uncomfortable.

"Uh—Miss Geraldine sent me over with gift baskets. There was some food I needed to put in the refrigerator."

The last time he'd seen her, she'd told him that she never wanted to see him again. Jubal was relieved to see her for any reason. He only wished she was happier to be here.

Pushing the brim of his black Stetson back a fraction on his forehead, he walked over to her. Here in the morning light, she seemed even more petite than he remembered. Her head would barely strike the middle of his chest, yet the curves hidden beneath her jeans and sweatshirt were all that he recalled and more. "I'm glad you brought them."

Stepping to one side of her, he poked through the items in one of the baskets on the tabletop. Angela tried to ignore his nearness, tried to pretend he still didn't look like the sexy cowboy she'd first fallen in love with when she'd been a mere nineteen years old. But she had to admit there was a sensuality about the man that she'd apparently forgotten and it was calling far too loudly to her now.

"Mmm, looks good," he said. "I'll have to thank Geraldine for being so thoughtful."

"I'll tell her you're pleased—as soon as I get back to the ranch house." Turning, she quickly started out of the room.

"Angie, wait."

Her heart hammering, she paused to look over her shoulder. For a moment, as her gaze skittered over his face, their eyes clashed and the brief meeting jolted her senses, reminding her of the wild, sweet taste of his kiss.

He cleared his throat. "The weather is miserable today. Why don't you take a minute to warm yourself at the fireplace?"

Was he trying to be thoughtful? Did he think being polite could wipe away the past, she wondered crazily. Forget that, Angela, she chided herself. Jubal doesn't want anything from you. Not now.

"That's hospitable of you, Jubal. Especially after—the things I said to you."

One of his shoulders lifted and fell. "You were upset,"

he explained. "I'm just glad you decided to see me for any reason."

She didn't know how to reply to that without raking up more of the past so she said, "I suppose I could stay for a few minutes."

Smiling faintly, he gestured toward the doorway and Angela preceded him out of the kitchen and into the living area.

The long room was filled with comfortable leather furniture and bright Navajo rugs. A snappy fire on the hearth radiated a welcome warmth.

For years she'd been haunted with the image of Jubal, Evette and their child sharing a home together. Now she had to rearrange those images and she wasn't at all sure how she felt about that. The wounded part of Angela had been happy to hear that Evette hadn't been able to hold on to him. But she wasn't happy about his losing the baby. The child had been an innocent victim in the whole affair. Just like Melanie.

Turning her back to the flames, she noticed that Jubal hadn't taken a seat. Seeing him standing so tall and strong in the middle of the room made her even more aware of the attractive picture he made and how vulnerable it made her feel to be alone with him.

"Did you know the family that lived here before?" he asked.

She nervously clasped her hands together. "No. They moved out before I had a chance to meet them."

"Geraldine told me that the man had respiratory problems and had to move to the western part of the state."

"Yes. Cook said everyone hated to see the family go."

Jubal nodded. "I get the impression that once a person

starts working here, he pretty much stays for life. Is that the way you feel?"

Was that his subtle way of asking about her plans for the future, Angela wondered. Or was he simply making conversation? Either way, it felt more than strange to be standing a few feet away from him, hearing his voice. For so long now he'd simply been a memory. Right now, she wasn't quite sure which was the best—the reality of being in his presence or the memory of being in his arms.

"I…right now I'm just concentrating on getting through the last of my college studies. This job is a blessing because Miss Geraldine allows me enough time to deal with my classes."

Interest flickered across his face. "Oh. You're still working on a college degree?"

Maybe at one time in her life, she'd behaved as though being his wife was going to be her career. Dear God, how humiliating. The two of them had only dated three months, yet Angela had already started planning a future with him. She'd been aware that he'd dated the mayor's daughter before her, but she'd truly believed that Evette was out of his life. He'd even insisted that the woman had only been someone to spend time with, not someone he seriously cared about. But then Evette had started making ugly noises, demanding that he come back to her. Jubal had refused. Then she'd announced she was pregnant, and everything had changed. Angela's life had changed.

Glancing away from him, she said, "Yes, I'm studying to be a teacher. But classes have broken for the semester right now."

Across the few feet of space separating them, she saw admiration in his green eyes. The reaction surprised her. It also made her think. Five years ago she and Jubal had been passionately involved, but they had not really known each other. Not in the way they should have.

"I didn't realize you wanted to be a teacher," he said. "I'm impressed."

She tried to tell herself that his compliment was hollow, that it meant nothing to her now. But she couldn't stop a tiny spurt of pleasure from spiraling through her.

Shrugging, she said, "I like working with children and I think the job will suit me."

"Elementary or high school?"

"Both, if I can pass the certification exam."

"You're a smart woman, Angie. You'll pass."

There it was, she thought with an inward groan. That endearing smile of his, the one that had once melted her heart, made her believe that she was the most special woman in his life. She couldn't let it affect her again. She had to be strong, had to remember that he couldn't be trusted. Ever.

"Well, that's a long way from now," she told him. "I still have another semester to go before I get my degree. And then I'll have to do my student teaching."

As the warmth of the flames seeped through her clothing, she noticed that everything about the house was nice and neat. That didn't surprise her. The Jubal she'd known had been a fairly tidy person. What did pique her curiosity was the absence of family photos. The only sign he even had a family at all was a small photo of his sister sitting on a nearby end table.

As she recalled, he'd been close to his family. Maybe he hadn't always agreed with them, but he'd loved them. As for Angela, the time she'd spent with the Jamisons had been brief and strained. They'd not exactly approved of their son's relationship with a much younger woman. Especially one from a poor background. But Angela had never blamed the Jamisons. She'd realized they were only looking out for their son's interests. Now she could only wonder if there had been a rift in the family.

"Well, I should be getting back to the ranch house, Jubal. Cook is waiting on me."

He cast her a pointed look. "You're in a big hurry to get away from me. I wonder what that means? That I'm getting under your skin, or that you hate the very sight of me?"

Stepping away from the warm hearth, she walked over to him. Her expression was as cool and distant as the high winter clouds and it chilled Jubal even more than the cold wind blowing across the Sandbur.

"Look, Jubal, I don't know what you're thinking, but I have no interest in starting things up—" her lips pressed together in a grim line "—where we left off."

Did he want to start things up with Angie? Jubal asked himself. A few days ago, he might have convinced himself that she was in the past and out of his life. But looking at her now, he was staggered by how much he wanted to start everything over with her.

"What would you say if I told you that I had an interest?"

For one brief second he saw her bottom lip quiver, but then a frown took the flash of vulnerable emotion away.

"That you're wasting your time," she said flatly.

For nearly five years he'd told himself to forget this woman, Jubal reminded himself, as his gaze wandered over her silky, brown hair, the rosy color staining her cheeks. He'd not searched for her because he'd figured she'd moved on and married someone else. He knew now that he'd made the wrong choice. He should have searched to the ends of the earth.

His throat thick, he said, "I don't blame you for hating me."

Her nostrils flared. "Hate is a mighty strong word, Jubal. And I like to think I'm not capable of hating anyone. But you—well, I just regret that I ever trusted you."

The groan inside him was so great Jubal couldn't stifle it. What could he possibly do or say to make up for the ugly mess he'd dragged her through?

Angela needs years of love and devotion, Jubal. Not just sweet words or kind acts.

Jubal realized the little voice in his head was right, but he also knew he had to try to fix things at the moment, otherwise, he'd never have a chance at anything long-term with this woman.

"Angie, God knows I didn't want to marry Evette. I didn't have much choice in the matter."

She stared at him so coldly that he glanced over his shoulder to see if the front door had jarred open and the chill racing down his spine was actually from the north wind.

"Jubal, I'm not nineteen anymore. I don't believe everything that spouts from a man's mouth. Especially yours. So don't insult my intelligence by trying to feed me a bunch of manure."

She didn't have to point out that she'd grown from the nineteen-year-old that had knocked him off his feet the first time he'd met her. She no longer looked at him with love and admiration. Now her eyes were full of mistrust and forced independence.

He raked a hand through his hair. "Angie, it ripped me apart to turn away from you and go to Evette."

She looked away from him. "Maybe it did. But you obviously managed to glue yourself together enough to marry her. And I—"

"I didn't have a choice!" he interrupted.

Her eyes bore down on his and he wondered how something as soft as sweet chocolate could look as hard as steel.

"The way I see it, you could have dealt with things differently. You could have offered her child support and help with raising the child," she said accusingly. "You didn't have to go so far as to marry her!"

Frustration clenched his jaw. "Everything in life isn't just right or wrong, black or white. And for your information, I tried giving Evette those options. She wouldn't hear of it. She kept insisting that she'd swallow a bottle of pills and end her life and the baby's."

Angela shook her head. "Evette was too in love with herself to do such a thing and you know it. She was the town princess. She refused to accept that there was anything she wanted that she couldn't have. And the baby was a convenient way of snaring you." She turned away from him and walked back to the fireplace. As she stared into the flames, she spoke in a raw, accusing voice, "When you and I first met, Jubal, I admired you for being honest with me about dating Evette. But you also assured me that your relationship with her had never been serious—and that it was over. Then I find out—"

"It *wasn't* serious! And as far as I was concerned, it was over."

Clearly aghast, she stared over her shoulder at him. "Not serious! You were making love to the woman!"

"That was before I met you. Not after. And having sex and making love is hardly the same thing," he countered defensively.

Sarcasm twisted her lips. "So that makes it okay."

"Nothing that happened to us was okay. But it would be better—for both of us, I think—if you could understand—"

"Well, I don't and I never will." She pulled her gloves from her pockets and began to jerk them on. "I've heard enough, Jubal. This is pointless. We were over long ago and rehashing everything is—"

Pushed by need, he walked over and curved his hands over the top of her shoulders. Instantly, her eyes closed and he watched her soft pink lips began to tremble once again. Everything in him longed to bend his head, to kiss away her pain. But he didn't want her to get the idea that the only thing he wanted from her was physical gratification.

Like heavy stones, regret lay in the pit of his stomach. "Angie—I never meant to hurt you."

"But you did."

She sounded shaken, accusing, bitter and Jubal was reminded all over again that the choices he'd made five years ago hadn't just affected his life. They had clearly impacted Angie in all the wrong ways and he couldn't feel any guiltier about that.

"I'm asking you to forgive me," he said lowly.

Angela's heart was racing out of control, urging her to run out the door as fast as she could, but her knees were too weak to move. And when he tugged her toward him, she fell awkwardly against his chest.

Planting her hands against his hard muscles, she pried enough space between them to allow her to look up at him. "Why should my forgiveness matter to you now, Jubal? Surely your conscience has gotten over abadoning me."

For one split second Angela believed she saw real torment on his face. Or was that just delusional wishing on her part?

"I've never gotten over you, Angie. Never."

Oh God, she wanted to believe him. Because, like it or not, she'd never been able to forget him. Even after he'd hurt her so badly, even after all these years, she'd not been able to turn off the memories of their time together.

"Please, Jubal—"

"Angie, there's something you need to know. The baby—Evette's baby—wasn't mine. After she miscarried, she confessed to me. The real father was a married businessman from Victoria."

His revelation struck her, numbing her with shock. "Oh, God! No!" she whispered hoarsely.

He nodded stiffly. "See, Angie, I was manipulated, lied to, betrayed. Evette only used me. When her lover refused to divorce his wife and marry her, she turned to her old boyfriend—me, the sucker that I was. I thought I was doing the noble thing. I wanted that child to have a real family. But in the end my efforts made no difference and I lost you in the process."

Crushed by the utter waste, the injustice of it all, Angela struggled to breathe, to even think. She had to get out of there and away from him before she broke into screaming sobs.

Quickly, without giving him a chance to stop her, she jerked away from his grasp and stumbled out the door. By the time she reached the truck and climbed inside, she was shaking all over. And as she quickly drove away, she didn't look back. She didn't want to know if he was watching her leave. The same way she'd watched him leave five years ago.

Driving back to the ranch house, Angela turned the heater on high and hoped the warm air would help her shivers subside. She didn't want Cook to see her in such a shaken state or have to explain why she and Jubal and Melanie weren't a family. It was simply too painful. Yet she had no doubt that Jubal would eventually see Melanie—their daughter—and then what? Would he put two and two together?

You've got to tell him, Angie. The man has lost a child he'd believed to be his. He had no way of knowing that at the same time you were carrying his baby. Even if he did hurt you, now more than ever, he has a right to know he has a daughter.

The voice inside her head was like a thorn in the heel. She couldn't move forward or backward without it hurting and she wondered how much more time would have to pass before she found the courage to finally pull it out.

Two nights later, Angela was sitting on the couch flipping through a text book for the coming semester, when Melanie, with an armload of storybooks, plopped down beside her.

"Read me a book, please Mommy? The one about the elephant that carries the sick little boy to the doctor."

Smiling indulgently, Angela reached to take the book from her daughter's grasp. "You like that story, don't you?"

Melanie's little head bobbed up and down. "Yeah! 'Cause the boy gets well. And everybody's happy—even the elephant."

"All right. Snuggle close so you can see the pictures," Angela instructed her as she helped her daughter scoot next to her side.

Thirty minutes later, she'd not only read the elephant story to Melanie, she'd gone through four more books and was about to start on the fifth. Then a knock sounded on the front door.

Excited at the idea of a visitor, Melanie jumped from

the couch and raced toward the door. "Somebody's here! Maybe it's Jess!"

"Mel, remember what I told you about opening the door? We have to see who's knocking first."

Jigging from one foot to the other, Melanie waited impatiently while her mother turned on the porch light and peeped out the small square window.

"Who is it, Mommy? Is it Jess?"

Shocked, Angela stared numbly at the man standing on the small porch, his back to the door. Even without seeing his face, she knew it was Jubal.

What was he doing on her doorstep, she wondered wildly. She'd not seen or spoken to him since she'd delivered the baskets to his house two days ago.

Darting a frantic glance at Melanie, she realized there was nothing to do but invite him in and hope he wouldn't recognize his own features on her little face.

"It's a friend," she finally said to Melanie. "So be on your best behavior. Okay?"

"I'm good, Mommy." Melanie's grin was nearly as wide as her face. "You know that."

Bracing herself, Angela opened the door and waited for Jubal to turn toward her. When he did, she was surprised to see a huge poinsettia plant in his arms and another box jammed under his arm. But it was the sexy grin on his face that really snagged her attention.

"Hello, Angela. I hope I'm not interrupting."

What could she say? That he'd interrupted her days, her nights, her very dreams for the past five years? No. Boiling the past over and over only cooked up a pot of trouble. She needed to deal with this man in a civil, impersonal way. But the flutter of her heart mocked that plan.

"You're not. Come in," she invited.

He was about to step over the threshold when he suddenly spotted Melanie's gamine face peeping curiously around her mother's pant leg. He smiled at the girl, then lifted a questioning gaze to Angela.

Her heart was pounding so hard and fast that she felt faint, but she somehow managed to shove the door wide and gesture for him to enter. Once he was inside the small living room, Angela quickly shut the door and turned to face him.

She sensed Melanie clinging to her side, waiting to see if the tall man with the big black hat was someone she wanted to get to know.

"I didn't expect you to be babysitting," he said. "I should have called first. But I figured you'd tell me not to come. So I invited myself."

Breathing deeply, Angela looked down at Melanie. There were so many things about Jubal that she could see in her daughter—*their* daughter—but hopefully, for tonight at least, he wouldn't recognize them.

"I…actually, I'm not babysitting, Jubal. Melanie is my daughter."

Chapter Four

Jubal stared at her in stunned silence. Then finally, after what seemed like ages, he seemed to collect himself.

"Your daughter," he repeated in stunned fascination. "I didn't realize—you never mentioned her."

Angela shrugged casually, but in reality she felt as though a volcano was erupting inside her. "It—the chance to speak of Melanie never came up."

The look Jubal slanted her said he doubted her excuse, but he didn't question her. Instead, he squatted to Melanie's height and offered the child his big hand.

Never one to shy away from strangers for long, Melanie plopped her tiny hand in his palm and tilted her head from side to side as she studied him candidly.

"What's your name?" she asked bluntly.

"My name is Jubal. And yours is Melanie?"

She nodded vigorously. "Melanie Jane Malone."

The last name must have caught his attention because he tossed a questioning glance up at Angela. She didn't answer. She couldn't. Seeing Melanie for the first time with her father had choked her with unshed tears.

Thankfully, instead of pressing Angela for explanations, he turned his attention back to Melanie. "That's a very pretty name," he told her.

"My mommy calls me Mel. Specially when she's mad."

Angela tried to smile, but tears were welling up in her heart, making her whole chest ache. Dear God, don't let me cry in front of my daughter, she prayed.

"I'll bet your mommy doesn't get mad too often, does she?" Jubal asked.

Melanie giggled, then shook her head. The movement sent her brown hair flying and she tucked it behind her ears as though she was a teenager instead of a four-and-a-half year-old.

"No. She's good! Really good!" To emphasize her point, Melanie flung her arms around Angela's thigh and hugged herself closer to her mother.

"I'll bet," Jubal said softly, then slowly rose to his feet.

Angela swallowed hard as he turned his green eyes on her. He was looking at her as though he were seeing her for the first time and the close inspection was shaking the floor beneath her feet.

Forcing herself to be mannerly, she gestured to the couch. "Uh—would you like to have a seat?"

He thrust the poinsettia at her. "Since Christmas is coming I thought you might like this."

The plant was full and lush, the velvety leaves a bright red. She'd never had a poinsettia before. There had always been too many necessities to buy at this time of year to splurge on plants. To think that Jubal had thought of her in this way sent soft emotions tumbling through her.

"It's very beautiful. Thank you." She took the flower from him and carried it over to a low coffee table in front of the couch.

"Here's something else, too," he said. "If Melanie has a sweet tooth, she might like these."

Angela placed the plant on the table, then turned to see him holding out a large box of fancy chocolates. Her questions about the reason for the two gifts must have shown on her face because he gave her a sheepish smile as she accepted the box.

"Thank you again, Jubal," she murmured.

Clearing his throat, he said, "I had planned to see you yesterday, but an emergency came up with a foaling mare and I couldn't leave her. I wanted to apologize for upsetting you when you came to my house the other day."

Upsetting her! She was still reeling from everything he'd told her. Evette hadn't given birth to Jubal's baby. She hadn't been pregnant with his child at all!

"What's in the box, Mommy? Can I have some, please?"

Shaking away her swirling thoughts, Angela guided her daughter over to the coffee table and selected three of the chocolates for Melanie. "It's candy," Angela told her. "And you may eat some after you thank Jubal."

Melanie promptly thanked their guest for the candy then sat on the floor to enjoy the treats. Angela turned to see that Jubal had taken off his jacket and hat and seated himself on the couch. He was making himself at home and that notion disturbed Angela. A part of her was terrified to have him around Melanie, worried that he'd recognize her as his daughter. Yet having him here felt oddly right somehow, as though he was filling an empty place in the house. Or was it an empty spot in her heart? Oh God, don't let me think like that, she prayed. Don't let me fall in love with the man again.

Extending the box toward him, she asked, "Would you like a piece?"

Smiling faintly, he leaned forward and picked out a square filled with caramel. "Sure. It's the time of year for eating."

She recalled his big appetite and thousands of other little things about him. Yet she realized they'd not spent a Christmas together and she wondered how much he threw himself into the holiday.

"Cook says Christmas has to be celebrated with your stomach, along with your spirit," she told him.

Angela placed the candy on the opposite end of the coffee table from Melanie, then took a seat two cushions down from Jubal.

"Smart lady," he agreed, then gestured toward the candy box. "Aren't you going to have any?"

Angela shook her head. "No. I had a big supper. Cook made pot roast and insisted I bring a bunch of it home with me."

"Cook," he repeated curiously. "I've met her. And I've been meaning to ask Lex if that is the woman's real name or just what everyone calls her."

"Her real name is Hattie Thibodeaux. I hear Miss Geraldine call her Hattie sometimes, but not often. She's quite a lady. I love her."

His green eyes studied her with quiet regard. "You say that as though you really mean it."

The light from a nearby table lamp shed a golden hue over his face and hair. Angela tried not to notice the light and dark streaks in his wavy hair, the rich amber flecks in his green eyes. Had he always been this handsome? Had just looking at him years ago made her heart beat as fast as it was beating now? Oh my, she wasn't supposed to be feeling like this. But she couldn't seem to make it stop.

Clearing her throat, she replied, "Cook has made coming here to the Sandbur extra special for me and Melanie."

Apparently Melanie was listening to the subject of their conversation, because she looked up and talked around the gooey lump of candy in her mouth. "Cook is my granny. She says she'll always be my granny. And she's pretty, too."

Jubal's expression softened as he glanced over at Melanie and Angela couldn't help but wonder how he'd dealt with Evette's miscarriage. She knew he'd wanted the best for the child. And she suspected that even if he'd known he wasn't the father, he would have raised him or her with just as much love. That much she *did* believe about Jubal.

To Angela he said, "I'm sure your parents are very proud of their granddaughter. Are you going to spend Christmas with them this year?"

Feeling as though a knife were in the middle of her chest, gouging a hole that would never mend, Angela stared down at her lap.

"No. At this time of year, the ranch has lots of parties. I won't have a chance to see my family."

Jubal frowned. "Surely Geraldine would give you some time off? She's not a taskmaster."

Not wanting him to think she was being overworked, she realized she was going to have to tell him the truth of the matter. At least, a bit of it.

"I shouldn't have used my work for an excuse. Geraldine is great to work for." She forced herself to look him squarely in the face. "I might as well tell you that I haven't seen my family in several years now. They…we had—well, you see, we're estranged."

If he was shocked by her admission, he didn't show it. The only change she could see in his expression was a faint narrowing of his eyes. "I can't believe that, Angie. What happened?"

You, she wanted to say. But she couldn't. If she so much as hinted that he was the reason for the tall wall between her and her parents, then he'd want to know why. And she simply wasn't ready to deal with telling the man that he had a daughter. Not just yet.

With a shallow sigh, she said, "You might remember how straitlaced my parents were. Well, that never changed. They have a narrow vision of how things should be. I—couldn't agree."

Angela realized the explanation sounded hollow. But she couldn't tell him that once her parents had learned she was pregnant with Jubal's child, they'd considered her a marked, scarlet woman and hadn't wanted the shame of her behavior to tarnish their righteous reputation. Her mother and father had ordered her to leave and expressed their wishes that she stay away from the family home until the sanctity of marriage had washed away some of her sins.

Angela didn't like to dwell on the memory of those lonely, frightening times, the struggle she'd gone through as she'd worked as a waitress through the heavy months of her pregnancy, how she'd scraped and forfeited to make a home for herself and her infant.

With a thoughtful frown, Jubal glanced away from her and over to Melanie, who was happily chewing one of the gooey chocolates. "It's a sad thing when families can't be together for Christmas."

Running her hands nervously down the thighs of her jeans, she hoped he couldn't see her struggling to swallow. Evette's lies to him about her child's parentage had been more than wrong, they had been devastating for all involved. So what did that make Angela for keeping Melanie's existence from him? Was she being just as much of a bitch? Until this moment, she'd always thought of herself as the victim. But now she had to reconsider that idea.

"Don't worry about it, Jubal. They know about Melanie and, believe me, they don't want either of us. I've accepted that and moved on. And as far as that goes, I don't want Melanie around that sort of narrow-mindedness." Angela quickly rose to her feet. "If you'll excuse me, Jubal, I'll go make coffee."

Jubal started to go after her, but decided now wasn't the time. So he sat staring at Angela's daughter, wondering about the man who'd fathered her. Where was he now? Why hadn't Angela married him? Or maybe she had and it had ended in divorce. In any case, it seemed totally ironic that at the same time Evette was supposed to have been having his child, Angela had given birth to another man's baby. Dear God, how unfair was that?

His mind was rolling those questions around when the little cherub across the room got to her feet and walked over to where he was sitting. He smiled at the child and she smiled back, then sidled up to his knee.

Jubal hadn't been around small children that much. His only sister, Carlotta, was older than him, so he'd not grown up with younger siblings and she didn't have any children of her own. A few of his friends back in Cuero had kids, but he'd not spent time with them. As he studied Angela's daughter, he was amazed at how tiny her hands were and the way her little bow-shaped mouth puckered as she gazed curiously back at him.

"Do you know how to ride a horse?" she asked.

"Yes. Do you?"

"No. But I can ride behind the saddle and hang onto Gracia's waist. She lets me do that sometimes. When she's being nice."

Gracia was Matt's and Juliet's daughter. When she wasn't at school, the teenager spent most of her time practicing on her cutting horses, but apparently she must take time once in a while to treat Melanie to a horseback ride.

Melanie shook back the brown ringlets framing her face and gave him another challenging stare. "Do you know how to read?"

Jubal very much wanted to chuckle, but he stifled the sound.

He didn't want to offend this perfect little angel. "Yes. Do you?"

Melanie giggled and Jubal thought how the sound was like tinkling Christmas bells. Joyful. Sweet.

"No, silly. I'm only four. I don't know how to read yet. But Mommy says I'll learn when I go to school."

"When will that be?" he asked, while thinking that Angela hadn't waited long to rebound into another man's arms. But he couldn't blame her for that. Not when he'd walked away and married Evette.

Melanie answered, "Next year I'll go to kinda—kinda-gotten."

"Hmm, kindergarten. Well, you'll learn a lot then."

She began to pat his knee as though she'd decided to like

him. Jubal was surprised at how much her little gesture touched him.

"Mommy says I'm a smart girl."

"I think your mommy is right."

Giggling again, she left his knee and began to gather a group of children's storybooks from the middle cushion of the couch.

"Will you please read me a story? I've heard 'em before," she confessed with adult-like candor. "But I like to hear 'em again."

She climbed onto the couch, wiggled next to his side and handed him the small stack of books. Jubal was so bemused by her trusting attitude toward him that he forgot he'd never done this sort of thing before or that if the cowboys down in the bunkhouse could see him, they'd probably all tease and call him daddy. None of them could know how very much he wished he'd fathered Angela's child.

Pushing that regretful thought away, he opened the first book on the stack. "Do you like this one?" he asked.

"Ooh yes!" she exclaimed with great drama. "It's about a pony and he's lost his tail. 'Cause a goat ate it off while he was asleep. And the pony thinks everyone is laughin' at him 'cause his tail is gone."

Jubal nodded. "I've seen that happen at least a dozen times."

Melanie's little features wrinkled with a look of disbelief. "You've seen a pony without a tail?"

"Sure. Sometimes goats eat things they shouldn't. Like horses' tails. But the pony's tail will grow back. Just like your curls would grow back if a little fairy ate them off."

Melanie giggled and plopped both hands on top of her head. "That's silly. No fairy will get my hair!"

Not if he could help it, Jubal thought. She was Angela's daughter and that made her even more precious. If she ever needed anything, wanted anything, he would be near to help. Even if her mother had other ideas.

Picking up the book, he began to read. "'Shadow was a shiny black pony with big brown eyes. He lived on a farm with all his friends and—'"

Minutes later, when Angela returned to the living room with coffee, Jubal was still reading and Melanie was asleep, her head resting in the crook of his big arm. For a moment she paused at the edge of the room. This was an image she'd dreamed about. Melanie and her father together, the way they should be.

But Jubal didn't know he was her father. And Melanie believed her father was just someone who'd chosen to live far, far away from them. Those facts were gnawing at Angela and filling the pit of her stomach with a sense of dread.

Trying to shake away her thoughts, she stepped forward. "I see Mel put you to work reading."

A half grin lifted one corner of his lips. "Yeah. Looks like she got tired. I didn't want to disturb her."

Angela placed a pair of steaming mugs on the coffee table. "I'll put her to bed."

"I'll do it," Jubal quickly offered. "Just show me where."

She looked up to see him shifting around on the couch and gathering Melanie up in the cradle of his arms. The child was limp, lost in dreamland with no idea that the big strong man who'd been reading her a story was now holding her.

Doing her best to shove the bittersweet thoughts aside, she guided Jubal to Melanie's bedroom where a night light shed a dim glow over the single bed. Near the foot, Mr.

Fields was asleep on a patchwork quilt. The cat didn't bother to lift his head.

Walking ahead of him, Angela picked toys from the floor and tossed them out of the way, making a clear walkway to the bed.

"Sorry the room is so messy," she apologized as she turned back the bedcover. "I usually make her pick things up before bedtime. But your company tonight interrupted her chores."

"Sorry about that. But as for the toys—at least your place looks lived in."

Meaning his didn't, she wondered. If Evette's child had lived he might have had toys and other kid items around the house. And if he'd known about Melanie? It was pointless for her to brood on that question now.

After he gently placed the girl on the sheet, Angela carefully tucked the quilt around her shoulders, then kissed her cheek.

When she finally turned away from the bed, she found Jubal watching her with a hungry sort of longing that pierced the very center of her.

Unable to speak, she simply gestured toward the door and he wordlessly preceded her out of the room.

Back in the living room, they both took up their coffee and settled a short distance from each other on the couch.

As Angela sipped her drink, she wondered what she could possibly say next. So many times she'd dreamed of the three of them living together as a happy family. What would he think if he knew how much she'd thought of him these past five years?

"This is a nice house," he said, breaking the silence. "The Sandbur families must really care about you."

Angela shrugged. She didn't like thinking that she'd been given special privileges over any of the other employees here on the ranch. She wanted to earn what she had, not have it given to her. Still, there was no denying that the Sandbar families had been good to her. "It's the nicest place Mel and I have ever had."

"So you like living here on the ranch?"

Nodding, she glanced around the room. Compared to his home, it was a bit cluttered, but the fact didn't embarrass her. Somewhere along the way of being banished by her parents and abandoned by the man she'd loved, she'd learned what was important in life and what was trivial.

"I'm glad for you," he said.

Beneath a veil of lashes, her gaze traveled over his long legs stretched in front of him, his tanned hand lying against his muscled thigh, the width of his broad shoulders beneath his starched shirt. He was as sexy as hell and every cell in her body seemed to be aware of it.

Forcing her gaze to the brown liquid in her cup, she asked, "What about you? You like living here?"

"Very much. The place is starting to feel like home."

Home. Yes, she was beginning to see that he'd come to the ranch needing a place to call home almost as much as she.

Watch it, Angie. You're not supposed to be having such soft feelings about Jubal. Not if you want to keep your heart safe.

Clearing her throat, she asked, "What about the clinic you had in Cuero?"

He shrugged. "Running it was very profitable, but even more stressful. Keeping good assistants isn't easy. Neither is working for the public. Here I don't have all those outside distractions. I can do what I really want to do—doctor sick animals and make sure they stay healthy."

Angela nervously crossed her legs, then uncrossed them. Tonight she was wearing old jeans and a denim shirt. No doubt he was thinking she'd turned dowdy since they'd parted. But would she have dressed more attractively if she'd known he was going to show up? Probably. If for no other reason than to show him what he gave up.

She said, "I figured by now the clinic was making you tons of money and that you were spending it all to keep Evette happy."

He let out a mocking snort. "Nothing could ever keep Evette happy. I thought it was me she wanted, but I turned out to be only half-right. Anyway, I don't really want to talk about her."

Angela could understand that. Most men wouldn't want to talk about a woman who'd connived, lied and trapped them into marriage.

Awkward moments stretched in silence. Angela could feel her palms growing damp, her heart thumping a bit harder. If he didn't go soon, she was going to break apart.

Finally, she said, "It surprises me that you moved away from your parents."

"I—don't really see them very much anymore. See, my parents weren't too happy about me divorcing Evette. They still believe that I should forgive her misdeeds. Hell, what do they think I am? An idiot?"

Angela shrugged. "She was the town's princess, Jubal. Being married to her made you the prince. Marrying someone like me would have crushed your parents. We both knew that."

He didn't bother to deny her words and frankly she was glad. To her, the truth was much better than any attempt to sugarcoat things.

Reality pushed a sigh past her lips as she rose from the couch and walked over to a pair of paned windows that looked out over the front lawn. From this vantage point she could see the lights of the Sanchez house about a quarter mile away. Between the houses, the wind was shaking the tree limbs, whistling through the cattle lots and picking up dust on the road. The night looked cold and lonely. The same way it had looked every night of her life since Jubal had walked away from her.

But now he was back, sitting in her house as though it were perfectly normal. What did it mean? Especially for Melanie. Was it time she revealed the truth to the both of them? Dear God, what was the right thing to do, she silently prayed.

"Angie."

The low whisper coming from close behind her momentarily stunned her and she stared straight ahead at the dark night, waiting with shallow breaths. For what? Another kiss? No! She couldn't give in to the man. But, oh heaven, how she wanted him.

"Jubal, I don't—think it was a good idea for you to come here tonight."

"Why?"

She groaned. "Because—nothing can come of it."

His hands rested on the tops of her shoulders and Angela felt herself melting from the warmth radiating from his fingers. "Angie, tell me about Melanie's father. What happened?"

She'd known this was coming. Even so, she wasn't prepared to answer.

Bending her head, she swallowed at the thickness invading her throat. "It—didn't work out. He was out of my life long before Melanie was born." That was certainly true enough, she thought sickly.

"He doesn't want to be a part of her life?"

"No," she said hoarsely.

She closed her eyes. What she truly wanted the most was for Melanie to have her father. But what would happen if she told him about her? He might possibly try to get sole custody, she thought frantically. And he had a good chance of getting it. Especially if a judge learned she'd kept Melanie's existence from Jubal for four-and-a-half long years.

"God, what a bastard!" he muttered.

Torn by his misguided reaction, she whirled around to face him. "Don't say that, Jubal!"

His nostrils flared. "Why? Because you still love the man?"

"Yes! No! Oh, Jubal, stop this!" she implored with a shake of her head. "It doesn't matter to you how I feel about Melanie's father. You just—have to get over this idea that there might still be a spark between you and me!"

His arms slid around her back and before she could resist he'd gathered her close against him. "Oh, Angie, I'd barely told you good-bye when I realized I made a terrible mistake—but at that time I'd felt so guilty about the baby. And later, after the divorce, I believed it was too late to go after you. Then when I saw you again the other night—I was stunned. I want to be close to you again. More than anything."

His voice was rough with emotion and it skittered over Angela's cheeks as his lips inched closer to hers. She felt herself wilting in response, desperately wanting to surrender to the desire that was beginning to grip her senses.

"I'm not that teenager that you seduced," she tried to reason.

His hands slid to the small of her back and tugged her hips against his. "No, you're a woman now. And I want to make love to that woman. The way I think you want to make love to me."

Just hearing him say the words thrilled her, scared her. Her heartbeat roared in her ears as hot color washed her cheeks. "How could you be so arrogant to think I want to make love to you again?"

"Because of this."

This was his lips closing over hers, searching out every curve, driving everything from her mind except the familiar taste of his kiss, the thrill of his hard body igniting tiny explosions inside of her.

Beneath the pressure of his lips, her mouth opened. As his tongue slipped inside, she felt a heavy fog of desire settling over her, muddling her senses. The resistance she had felt only moments before was crashing in broken bits at her feet. All she wanted was to get closer to the man, to feel the strength of his arms around her, the hardness of his body filling hers with paralyzing need.

Jubal had been her one and only lover. And not until this moment had she realized how empty and hungry she'd become without him. His touch, his warmth was consuming her, turning her into a woman again.

As his lips dominated hers, she was vaguely aware of his hands roaming against her back, tangling in her hair, then finally moving to the front of her shirt. When his fingers closed around the button between her breasts, reality flipped on a warning bell in her head. The embrace was taking her to a place she couldn't allow herself to go. No matter how much she wanted him to take her there.

Mustering all the resistance she could find, Angela

finally managed to tear her lips from his and move back from him, until the cold window panes were pressing against her shoulder blades, blocking her escape.

"You'd better go, Jubal," she whispered hoarsely. "Now!"

His hand reached beseechingly toward her. "Angie, what we had together—it's not over. I can feel it and I know you do, too."

Whirling around to put her back to him, she bent her head and bit down hard on her trembling lip. "Wanting each other doesn't make it okay. Not with me. I don't trust you. Not now—or ever!"

"Have you ever heard of the word *forgiveness,* Angie?"

She was wondering how she could possibly answer that question when she heard the front door open and close.

Glancing around, she saw that he was gone. But not his presence, she thought, helplessly. It would hang around to haunt her.

Chapter Five

Jubal's house was roomy, the furniture handpicked for comfort and durability, the kitchen filled with plenty of cabinets and nice appliances. Even the fireplace was a luxury he was enjoying on these cold December nights. Yet the house was missing something, and until he'd gone to Angela's last night, he'd not known what that something was.

Now he did. It was missing a family. A child's clutter. A woman's soft touch.

The hollow sound of his boots against the shiny parquet flooring followed him as he walked to the kitchen and opened the refrigerator. Normally he ate lunch at the bunk house with the cowboys and that's where he should have been right now. Their chatter might have distracted his thoughts from Angela.

Ever since Jubal had left her house, his mind had been vacillating back and forth between their heated kiss and the fact that she had a daughter. A daughter old enough to walk and talk and charm the socks right off of him.

He didn't know why learning about Melanie had shocked him so. Once they'd parted he'd gone on with his life and Angela had certainly had every right to go on with hers. So why had Melanie's existence shaken him?

Deep down, he had to admit that he felt cheated. Angela and Melanie should have been his. Instead, his house and his heart were empty.

Minutes later, Jubal was gnawing on a piece of cold fried chicken, wondering how he could possibly approach Angela again, when his cell phone rang. Seeing that it was Matt on the other end of the line, he quickly flipped the instrument open and answered, "Hey, Matt. Anything wrong?"

"I think Misty Girl is trying to foal. Since this is her first baby, I thought you ought to be close by."

"I'm glad you called. I'll be right there."

Snapping the phone shut, he reached for his jacket and hurried out of the house. Yet as he drove to the ranch yard, it wasn't Misty Girl that was worrying him. It was Angela. He wanted another chance with her. He wanted to spend the rest of his life making up for the hurt he'd caused her. But how could he ever convince her of that?

Angela was in the kitchen when Geraldine stuck her head around the door.

"Misty Girl has had her colt!" she announced with a proud grin. "Get Melanie and go take a look at him."

Angela had learned that if the boss lady thought it was time to play, then everything else was put on hold, so she didn't argue. Instead she and Melanie donned thin jackets and headed off to the horse barn.

It was a warm, lovely day and Melanie showed her joy in being outdoors by skipping and dancing her way to their destination.

"Mommy, does the colt have a new name? Can I name him?"

"I'm sure the new colt has already been given a name." Misty Girl was one of the Sandbur's top cutting mares. Geraldine had been looking forward to this birth for months now and no doubt, she'd gone to great pains to pick out a name for the new foal.

Melanie spun a few pirouettes. "Oh. Well, can we tell Jubal about the new baby?"

Angela tried not to sigh. Ever since Jubal's short visit the previous night, Melanie had done nothing but talk about the man.

"He already knows about the new baby. He might have even helped it get born," Angela said. All the way down here, she'd had her fingers crossed that Jubal wouldn't be around. She wasn't ready to face him. Not after that kiss they'd shared. For a few moments, they'd been fused together like hot, forged iron. In fact, she was still wondering where she'd found the scrap of will power to pull away from him.

"Oh. Did he help me get born?"

Her daughter's innocent question brought a sudden sting of tears to Angela's eyes, but she quickly blinked them away and reached to open the barn door.

"No, darling," Angela gently answered. "Jubal lived somewhere else when you were born."

Inside, the cavernous building was lit by sunshine streaming through the skylights scattered at intervals across the ceiling far above them. The pungent scent of hay and pine shavings mixed with the smell of horses and leather.

As Angela and Melanie walked along the wide alleyway, several stalled horses hung their heads over half gates and watched them with curious stares.

"Mommy, can we stop and pet the horses? Please?" Melanie begged. "And give them sugar cubes?"

"We didn't bring sugar cubes. And we came to see the baby horse, remember?"

"Okay! Let's go, Mommy! Hurry!"

Melanie took off in a run, but Angela promptly caught her by the hand.

"No running, young lady," Angela ordered. "You might scare the horses."

Understanding her mother meant business, Melanie walked obediently by Angela's side until they reached a wooden fence that cordoned off the foaling area. The first four feet of the tall fence was solid boards, in order to keep any mothers and babies from getting their legs or heads stuck between the slats.

Angela was about to lift her daughter up to see the animals on the other side of the fence, when Jubal's voice sounded behind them.

"No need for that," he said. "I'll take Melanie inside for a closer look."

Turning, Angela watched his rapid approach. Dressed in faded jeans and a frayed denim shirt with pearl snaps, he looked sexier than ever. From the grin on his face, he didn't appear to be hanging on to any anger over their confrontation last night and she wondered if he'd forgotten she'd told him that things were well and truly over between them. She certainly hadn't forgotten. The words had ripped her apart and she was still trying to make her heart believe she'd meant them.

"Miss Geraldine thought Mel might want to see the new baby," she explained.

After running a pointed look over Angela, he turned his attention to Melanie, who'd turned away from the fence and was now eyeing him with a wide grin.

"Hi, Jubal!"

"Hello yourself," he replied.

Quickly, she moved forward and clasped her two hands around his big one. "I wanta see the baby. Is he pretty?"

Bending, Jubal touched a finger tip to her freckled nose. "Not as pretty as you. But he'll do." Reaching for the girl, he swung her up into his arms. "Let's go have a look."

"Yay! Yay!" she squealed.

"Sssh!" Angela quickly quietened her with a finger against her lips. "You have to be quiet, Mel, so as not to scare the little fellow."

Jubal glanced over at Angela and her heart began to pound as her gaze skittered over his face and landed on his lips. Thank God, she thought, he couldn't see inside her to know how very much she wanted to kiss him again.

"Want to come along?" he invited.

She swallowed. "No thanks. I'll watch from here."

He didn't press her. Instead he walked around the circle of fence until he reached a gate.

Angela couldn't help but notice how trusting Melanie was with the man and how naturally her little hand rested on his big strong shoulder as he carried her into the pen. She couldn't help but see the tender, fatherly way he treated Melanie, and the image was so bittersweet, she deliberately turned her attention to the gray mare and little black colt by her side.

Ten minutes later, Angela announced that their visit

with the baby was over. But much to her dismay, Jubal seemed intent on ambling along with them as they headed back down the alleyway.

"Mommy, can we see the big horses now? Can we?"

Melanie started to skip ahead of them and Angela immediately started to call her back, only to have Jubal stop her.

"Don't spoil her fun," he said. "She won't hurt anything."

Angela looked doubtfully from him to Melanie, who was already heading toward a paint horse that was nickering softly at the little visitor.

"The horses might bite her," Angela voiced her fears.

Jubal smiled faintly. "Not this gentle bunch. They understand that she's a baby and needs to be watched over."

Still unconvinced, she said, "If you say so."

He moved closer to her side. "I do."

If she had any sense at all, Angela thought, she'd pick up the pace and get herself and Melanie out of there as fast as she could. But her daughter was having such fun. Plus, Angela didn't want Jubal to get the idea she was afraid to be in his presence. So she kept her feet moving at a slow stroll, as though spending time with him here in the barn was as normal as the sun rising in the east every morning.

"Angela, about last night—"

Every nerve in her body stiffened. "Let's not talk about that, Jubal."

"Okay. I'll move on to something else. I'd like for us to go out on a date."

Stunned by this turn in the conversation, Angela stared up at him. "A date! You're kidding!"

He shrugged. "Why would I be?"

"Be-because," she stuttered. "What good could come out of a date? We'd end up arguing."

A sexy little grin twisted his lips. "Or maybe we'd wind up in each other's arms," he murmured.

He moved a bit closer to her side and Angela drew in a long breath as her heart kicked into higher gear. Common sense said that she shouldn't allow herself to be the least bit attracted to this man. But somewhere between last night and now she seemed to have lost her common sense. "I—doubt that."

"Why? It happened before."

Angela silently groaned. It was all too easy to recall Jubal making love to her, touching her body and heart so deeply that he'd forever changed her life. Would she be crazy to let him in her life again? To think that this time it might actually work?

"Yes. But it won't happen again," she said, trying her best to sound firm.

"If you're so sure about that, then a little date with me isn't going to hurt anything," he countered.

How could she argue that point?

She sighed. "I didn't come down here to the barn for this, Jubal. I came to see Misty's new baby."

"That doesn't matter. Even if I hadn't seen you today, I would have asked you later."

After glancing around to make sure Melanie was okay, Angela faced him. "Why, Jubal? Five years have passed since you chose to make a life with Evette. Not once during that time did you try to contact me. I wasn't far away. If you'd really wanted to find me, you could have."

A grimace passed over his features. "Angela, the idea of looking for you went through my head most every day. But I fought the urge."

Each time she thought she couldn't be hurt any more by

this man, he said something that stabbed her right down to the bone. "Why? Because of Evette?"

He rolled his eyes toward the hayloft far above their heads. "Hell, no! Because of you. I believed that—well, I thought that you'd probably already married someone else." His gaze settled back on her face. "I'd caused you enough problems. If you were happy, I didn't want to interfere."

Five years ago she'd gobbled up his affectionate promises like a hungry hound. But he'd broken his promises and she didn't know how she could ever believe anything he said to her again.

Carefully avoiding his gaze, she asked, "What makes you think I don't have another man in my life?"

"You're not married," he pointed out.

Since they'd parted, Angela had told herself that she needed to move on and find a man she could love, a man to be a father to Melanie. But each time she'd tried to look at a man in a romantic way, Jubal's memory had blocked her efforts. Now he was no longer a memory. He was real and by her side and she couldn't seem to stop the flood of longing his nearness evoked.

Feeling desperately vulnerable, she turned her head away from him. "I could have a boyfriend."

His thumb and forefinger wrapped around her chin and urged her face back to his. "Do you?"

Whenever he touched her, it was as though time had never passed. The same longing, the same electric excitement rushed over her like flood water racing over a dry, barren field. In spite of herself, she welcomed it, soaked it up like a thirsty flower.

Forcing her gaze on his green eyes, she said, "No. My track record with boyfriends isn't all that great."

"Apparently Melanie's father wasn't an honorable man," he said with a measure of regret. "And I'm sorry that I wasn't either."

She inwardly stiffened. She'd forgotten that Jubal believed there had been another man in her life—Melanie's father. Oh God, that's what happens when a person tells a lie, she thought ruefully. One called for more and more. When was she going to find the courage to stop it?

Her throat tightened with emotions. "I don't want to talk about him—or any of that."

"Neither do I. We were discussing a simple date. Let's both stay on track here."

Oh how she wanted to stay on track, but Jubal Jamison had always made her veer off course. Still, going on a date with Jubal would give her an opportunity to find out if he was merely flirting or if he truly wanted something more serious from her. Either way, before she would even give him a hint that Melanie was his daughter, she needed to know if he was a different man from the one that had easily tossed her away. Because this time, she had more than herself to protect. There was no way she was going to give him the chance to break Melanie's little heart.

"All right, Jubal," she said suddenly. "I'll go on a date with you."

For a moment he looked completely stunned. Then he laughed as though she'd just made him a very happy man. The sound tugged on her heart and she suddenly realized that pleasing him made her feel far better than cutting him with bitter barbs.

"Wow! I wasn't expecting that," he said. "I figured I'd have to get on my knees and beg."

"I don't like to see a man beg for any reason." And in spite of all he'd done to her in the past, he was no exception.

Turning forward, she began to walk toward Melanie and he quickly fell into step at her side.

"I'll pick you up tomorrow evening about six," he said.

"I'll be ready," she told him. Yeah, who was she kidding, she wondered. She could never be ready for Jubal.

Thankfully, the next day was quiet on the ranch. Angela had so little to do that Cook insisted she go home early.

"There's no need for that," Angela said as she puttered around the kitchen in the big ranch house. "It's not like I'm going on some special outing."

Cook snorted as she shuffled the deck of cards she'd been using to play solitaire. "I imagine going out with Dr. Jamison would be special for most any young lady like yourself. He'd be quite a catch."

Angela peeped into the oven at the casserole that Cook was preparing for Geraldine's supper. "I don't want to catch the man, Cook."

"Then what are you going out with him for? You told me the other day that you didn't want to have anything to do with the man."

She shut the oven door. "I didn't. I don't." She threw up her hands in a helpless gesture. "I mean, nothing serious is going to come out of this, Cook. It's just a simple date."

One by one, Cook began to lay the cards on the work table. "Hmm, strange way to show a man you don't like him."

Untying the apron from around her waist, Angela said, "I want him to get the message that he's wasting his time pursuing me. Spending a little time with me will show him that I'm not the same girl he remembers."

"You mean the same girl he fell in love with?"

Moving down the cabinet, Angela pretended an interest in a recipe that was propped against a large canister of flour. "Cook, Jubal never fell in love with me. He said he did—but he couldn't have. He married someone else and I became the forgotten woman."

A few moments passed in silence and then Cook came to stand next to Angela, placing a bony hand on her shoulder.

"I'm not normally a nosy woman, Angie," she said gently. "And you don't have to tell me anything else about you and the doc. I'm just trying to tell you to be careful, that's all."

Closing her eyes, Angela swiped a hand through her tumbled hair. "Does living carefully make a person happy, Hattie?"

Cook's hand gently patted her back. "I don't know, honey. I lost my man and could never find another. Maybe you've been given a second chance, hmm?"

With a tiny sob catching in her throat, Angela turned and hugged Cook close. "I'm not sure I believe in second chances."

When Jubal drove up in front of Angela's house that evening, she was ready and waiting. With Melanie safely ensconced for the night with Juliet and Matt, all she had left to do was pull on her coat and grab her handbag.

A glow from the porch light lit the walkway and as she approached the yard gate, she could see Jubal waiting there to greet her.

"Good evening," he said, pressing a kiss on her cheek as though the two of them had never been apart.

Dimples bracketed her lips as he opened the little gate,

then shut it behind them. "Getting a little familiar, aren't you?" she playfully teased in an effort to hide just how much the simple display of affection had touched her.

Chuckling, he touched a fingertip to the spot where he'd kissed her cheek. "A kiss on the cheek? I saw Lex kiss you on the cheek the night of the party. Was he getting familiar?"

Her cheeks warmed with color. "Lex kisses all women on the cheek. It's just his nature."

"Sure it is," he drawled.

When they reached his pickup truck, he helped her into the passenger side before climbing into the driver's seat. As Angela fastened her seatbelt, she fully expected him to start the engine and drive away. Instead, he switched on the cargo light and reached across her to open the glove compartment.

The scent of him, the nearness of his body rattled her senses, but she did her best to sound casual as she asked, "What's the matter? Lost something?"

"I hope not," he murmured.

Long, agonizing moments passed while he fished through the jumble of items in the small compartment. Then finally to her great relief, he pulled back to his side of the seat.

"Here. This is for you." He handed her a small box covered in red foil with a satin bow. "Open it."

Bemused, she stared at the shiny package. She'd not expected anything like this. But then, she'd never dreamed she'd be going on a date with him, either. "Jubal, this wasn't part of the deal."

Smiling with faint amusement, he said, "We didn't make a deal. And before that pretty little head of yours starts working overtime, I'm not trying to buy your affections. That's just a trinket for the holiday season."

She didn't want to appear ungrateful by refusing the gift.

Besides, she thought, making an issue over it would seem ridiculous and give the whole thing too much importance.

Slipping off the green satin ribbon, she tore into the paper until she reached a white box. Feeling as excited as though it really was Christmas, she pulled off the lid and stared down at a rhinestone pin shaped like a horse. Around its neck was a wreath fashioned with green and red stones. The pin was beautiful and she had the odd feeling that it was a bit more than an inexpensive piece of costume jewelry, but she kept the notion to herself.

Lifting the broach from its velvet bed, she whispered, "Jubal, it's precious."

"Let me pin it to your coat."

Taking the horse from her, he positioned the piece of jewelry against the left shoulder of her wool jacket. The stones glistened against the off-white fabric and for a moment, Angela felt like a princess, a woman worthy of a man's attention.

"How's this?" he asked.

She didn't care where he pinned it, as long as he hurried and finished the task. With his head bent close to hers, she could do nothing but stare at the thick waves of his sandy brown hair, draw in the spicy, masculine scent emanating from his body and think about the way his lips had felt against hers. The way they could feel again if she invited him to kiss her.

Biting down on her lip, she closed her eyes and tried to think of anything but him.

"There," he said, finally straightening away from her. "Looks pretty to me. Okay with you?"

Her hand trembling, she reached up and touched the tip of her forefinger to the edge of the broach.

"Very pretty," she said huskily. "Thank you, Jubal."

His hands paused on the steering wheel as he gently studied her. "I think you mean that," he said in a low voice.

Her throat was suddenly so thick that she had to swallow before she could reply. "I do mean it."

He smiled. "Good. I've got something special planned for tonight."

Was she dressed for special, she wondered. A black circle skirt of suede-like fabric and a black turtlenecked sweater looked respectable, but hardly appropriate for anything fancy.

Nervously, she crossed her legs and smoothed the hem of her skirt over her knee. "I thought we were going out to dinner."

He backed out of the drive and headed the truck toward the ranch yard. "We are. But we're going to the theater first."

Angela tried to hide her disappointment. She had never been a movie watcher. She wouldn't know one actor from another.

"Oh."

Her lackluster response prompted him to look over at her. "Not the movies. The theater—with live actors."

Intrigued now, she turned slightly in her seat to face him. "Really? I've never been to the theater. Not ever."

"Then I'm glad I'm the one taking you."

Reaching across the seat, he squeezed her hand, and there was something on his face that said he wanted to give her more than a pleasant evening out. He wanted to love and care for her.

The idea shook her to the center of her being. Was this the true side of him, or was she merely seeing what she wanted?

* * *

The theater performance turned out to be a musical with singers and dancers portraying the big band era at Christmastime. It was full of lively, rollicking tunes and by the time Angela and Jubal left the the community theater, she was in a very happy mood that spilled over into their quiet, Italian dinner.

"The food is delicious, Jubal," Angela remarked as she forked some ravioli into her mouth. "Just don't tell Cook I said that, though. It might hurt her feelings."

Without asking, the hostess had put them in a private alcove, further secluded by a potted palm. Angela was acutely aware that they were separated from the rest of the diners and that Jubal's shoulder was close to hers. He would hardly have to lean at all to place a kiss on her lips.

"Do you mostly work with her in the Saddler house?"

Trying to shake away her erotic thoughts, she answered, "Yes, making sure the maids have everything clean and the laundry taken care of—things like that. But I think Miss Geraldine mostly wants me to make sure that Cook doesn't overdo it."

"I don't figure Cook wants to be coddled," he said wryly. "She seems like an independent cuss to me."

Angela nodded. "That's true. But she seems to like my company. And she loves Mel. I guess since she doesn't have any children of her own."

"I think Melanie would be special to anyone. She's an adorable little girl."

And she's yours, Jubal. She's your daughter. Oh God, what would you think if I told you?

Shoving that tormenting question away, she smiled wanly. "By the time I pick Melanie up from Juliet and

Matt's in the morning, they'll be wishing they'd never offered to babysit for me," she joked. "But Jess loves to play with her and thankfully the maids help corral the children."

His green eyes glanced up from his plate to settle suggestively on her face. "Melanie is staying over with the Sanchezes tonight? I thought they were only watching her until you got home."

Her heart thumped faster. Was he thinking about spending the night with her? Did he know how much she was thinking about it?

She drew in a long breath and slowly released it. "Jubal, that doesn't mean you should be getting any ideas."

Like a lazy fingertip, his sexy chuckle rippled down her spine.

"I'd never do that, Angie. I'm just thinking it will give us time to go to my house for a little dessert before I take you home."

His house? Oh my, she was headed for trouble.

"Dessert?" she questioned inanely. "Don't they serve it here?"

His lips twisted to one of those smiles that had been Angela's undoing five years ago.

"Not the kind I have."

Chapter Six

Fifteen minutes later, when Jubal suggested they leave the restaurant, Angela didn't argue. After all, to linger over a dinner they'd already finished wouldn't make sense. Still, she wasn't sure that she felt good about going to Jubal's house for dessert—even if he really had something.

Still, his company was an indulgence she didn't want to give up. At least, not yet. It was nice, so nice, to simply pretend that this man beside her had always really loved her. That he'd never chosen another woman over her.

"Jubal, are you sure you even have anything in your house that remotely resembles dessert?"

He laughed as he steered the truck onto the Goliad Highway. "Sure I do. Italian cream cake. A huge one."

"Jubal!" she scolded. "We just left an Italian restaurant. They probably had that on the menu."

"No. They didn't. I looked. Besides, it wouldn't taste as

good as this one. A lady sends me a huge homemade cake every year around this time. I did surgery on her dog after he'd been hit by a car and she's never quit thanking me for saving his life."

"Hmm. Must be nice to be remembered and appreciated."

He tossed a faint scowl at her. "You say that like you don't have anyone. That can't be true. I've always remembered and appreciated you."

Maybe he had thought of her, she conceded. But thinking of her wasn't the same as searching for her, or trying to contact her. Thinking of her didn't make up for Melanie not having a father.

But whose fault is that, Angie? You should have told Jubal you were expecting. You should have given him a choice as to whether he wanted to be a father to Melanie.

The little voice brought her up short and reminded her bluntly that she'd not handled things in the best of ways, either. She should have considered Jubal's feelings, too, rather than simply acting on what she thought best for herself and Melanie.

With a silent sigh, she purposely headed their conversation in a different direction. "Actually, Jubal, I was talking about your work as a vet. Most people are very attached to their pets. They probably see you as their savior."

With a wry shake of his head, he said, "I wouldn't put me on that high a pedestal."

"I recall how impressed my father was with you when you came out and doctored our goat."

Surprised that she'd brought up that part of their past, he glanced her way. "You still remember the day we first met?"

She nodded. "The little fellow was very sick. You said

he had something like Coccid—" She gave up trying to pronounce the medical term and said, "Whatever it was, you said he could spread it to the rest of the goats."

"Coccidia. Yeah, I guess you were paying attention that day." His voice softened as he added, "What I recall the most about that day is the pretty young girl in tight blue jeans with a bandanna tied around her long brown hair."

The only response she made to his remark was to gently clear her throat. Jubal realized with sudden clarity that in many ways he was still causing her pain. And that was the very last thing he wanted to do.

Reaching across the seat, he covered her hand with his. "I was probably too old to be looking at you that day—the way a man looks at a woman. But I don't regret that now."

"I was nineteen and you were thirty," she said softly. "You always believed the difference in our ages was a problem—but it wasn't the real problem."

Jubal had to admit that she was right. Whenever they'd been together, it had been hard for Jubal to remember their age difference. He'd been too in love with her, too selfish to stop and consider what he might be doing to her young, innocent heart.

Dear God, he could still remember how she'd looked when he'd told her about his decision to marry Evette. The utter disappointment on her face had cut him to the core. And, sadly, he still saw that look of disappointment in her eyes. It was a look he desperately wanted to change to love and pride.

But how? It was miraculous that she was forgiving enough just to be sitting here next to him. She'd told him in clear terms that everything between them was over.

But when he'd kissed her, those words hadn't rung true.

He'd tasted longing and need on her lips. Or was that only wishful imagining on his part?

"You're right. I was the real problem. I was a fool for getting involved with Evette in the first place. And I should have never believed her about the baby."

Even though his eyes were on the highway, he could feel her head lift, her gaze travel over his profile.

"Jubal, you can tell me the truth now," she said in a low, hoarse voice. "Did you—did you make love to her after you met me?"

The misery in her voice made him want to stop the truck and pull her into his arms. "Angie, I never was a kid that liked to peel scabs off of an old wound. Nothing can heal if you make it bleed over and over."

"Not knowing the truth makes me bleed," she countered.

He groaned. "I've told you the truth. After I met you, I never touched the woman. You and I dated for three months. When Evette came to me and told me she was pregnant, she was already four months into her pregnancy. Do the math. I thought there was a possibility I could have been the father. Little did I know that she'd been seeing another man in Victoria. But let's forget about all those old wounds tonight," he suggested. "Let's try to enjoy the rest of the evening. Okay?"

Long moments passed before he heard her release a small sigh.

"Okay, Jubal. I don't want our night to be ruined."

By the time they reached Jubal's house, a light rain had begun to fall. Jubal took off his jacket and insisted Angela use it to hold over her head as they sprinted to the porch.

"It's getting cold," Angela remarked through chattering teeth as he opened the front door and ushered her inside.

"It won't take but a minute or two to get the fire stoked up," he assured her.

After switching on a couple of table lamps, Jubal went straight to the fireplace and piled on several more logs from the wood box. While he tended to the fire, Angela hung Jubal's jacket on a nearby hall tree, then took off her own coat and hung it next to his.

"I have the central heat going, too," he spoke up. "If you'd like for me to turn up the thermostat, I will."

She moved closer to the warmth of the flames. "I'm fine now that I'm out of the wind," she assured him.

Satisfied with the fire, Jubal placed the screen back on the hearth, then gestured toward the couch and armchair. "Make yourself comfortable, Angie. I'm going to the kitchen after the cake and coffee."

He started out of the room and she quickly called after him. "Do you need help?"

Pausing at an open doorway, he glanced back at her and smiled. "You spend enough time in the kitchen. Let me wait on you for a change."

As she watched him disappear from sight, Angela couldn't help thinking that Jubal was caring for her like a princess. Just as he had when they'd been together for those brief months five years ago. Back then, Jubal had always treated her with gentleness and respect, as though she was the most precious thing on earth to him. And she was beginning to see that that hadn't changed; he was still treating her with respect. But would it last? Could it last?

Thoroughly warmed by the fire, she stepped away from the hearth and began to meander around the room. When Jubal reappeared, she was inspecting a small bronze sculpture of a bucking horse. As he placed a tray of refreshments on a nearby table, he slanted a glance her way.

"Come sit down," he invited. "The coffee is hot and strong."

She followed him over to the couch and took a seat at the end. His presence was bigger than the room and as he bent near to hand her one of the steaming mugs, along with a saucer full of cake, she could feel her insides quivering in reaction to his closeness. Sitting in a restaurant with soft music in the background and candles on the table had been hard enough on her senses, but here on this isolated spot of the ranch, with no one around except a herd of cows, it was impossible to keep her mind away from the desire that was beginning to simmer deep inside her.

After gathering up his own cake and coffee, he sat down on the cushion next to hers and watched intently as she picked up her fork and cut off a tiny bite.

Fighting the urge to squirm, she said, "You're supposed to be eating, not watching me."

"I'm waiting to see how you like the cake." Dimples marked his cheeks as he added, "Besides, you look so beautiful tonight that I can't quit staring at you. It would be inhumane to make me stop."

Don't take the man seriously, she told herself. But her heart was soaking up his words, storing them away like treasured gems. "I see you haven't forgotten how to flirt."

Leaning closer, he touched a finger to the dip between her nose and her upper lip. "It's easy with you," he said softly.

Heat flooded her cheeks, then stormed a path all the way to the soles of her feet. Her heart was humming, urging her to get closer, while her mind was yelling at her to jump up and run.

Turning her head just enough to evade his touch, she murmured, "Eat your cake, Jubal."

He eased back from her, although the sensual glint in his green eyes remained. "You're no fun at all," he teased.

He was right about that, Angela thought. Being a single mother with little money and no family to help had changed her whole outlook on life. The laughing, happy young woman who'd first fallen in love with Jubal had turned into a practical, serious soul.

Forcing herself to lift a bite of cake to her lips, she said huskily, "You don't have to tell me that I've gotten pretty boring, Jubal."

His hand wrapped around her forearm. "I was only teasing, Angie," he said gently.

Why, oh why, did he look at her that way, she wondered. As though she were special, as though he actually cared about her. Was she looking at him clearly, or was the emptiness inside her clouding her vision?

"I know you were. But I wasn't. I'm not—" She drew in a deep breath and began again, "That same fun girl you used to know. But then I guess you've already discovered that for yourself."

The faint smile on his face disappeared as his fingers began to move back and forth against her arm. The simple touch caused goose bumps to erupt across her skin, telling him just how strongly he was affecting her.

"Years have passed," he told her. "I don't expect you to be that teenager I first met on your parents' farm."

Certain she was treading toward slippery ground, Angela pulled her arm from his grasp and glanced around the room. "Are you going to put up a Christmas tree this year?" she asked in an effort to change the subject.

His gaze followed hers. "I hadn't really thought about it. Mother used to decorate for Christmas, but I've never done it since I've been on my own. What about you?"

For the first time since they arrived at his house, a genuine smile lit her face. "Of course. Mel will be expecting Santa to visit her. And there has to be a tree for the jolly old elf to leave gifts under."

He smiled. "So Melanie believes in Santa Claus and all that stuff?"

Angela nodded. "I wouldn't want it any other way. That's the most special part of being a kid. Make-believe. The excitement of waiting for Santa's visit. Waking up the next morning to find the tooth fairy has left money under the pillow. I never got any of that, Jubal. And I don't want my daughter to miss out."

Clearly surprised, he asked, "Your parents didn't celebrate Christmas? That's hard to imagine. Especially with them being so religious."

Angela grimaced. "Oh, they celebrated Christmas. They just didn't do the Santa thing or reindeer and sleigh bells. You get the picture. As for the tooth fairy, Dad considered it evil if I even mentioned anything to do with trolls or fairies or fantasy things. He believed that sort of frivolity led to a person's downfall."

Shaking his head with dismay, Jubal said, "I remember Oscar being a little stern. But I don't remember you bringing up any of this about the man."

Angela winced. Even though their affair had lasted nearly four months and produced a daughter, there were still many things they didn't know about each other. Maybe they'd spent so much time making love that they'd overlooked the most important form of communication—talking.

"I didn't want to tell you about my parents' strict beliefs," she said softly. "Those sorts of things—well, they're embarrassing for a girl to discuss with a boyfriend."

"I wish you had talked to me about your father—your parents." His voice lowered as his hand slid up her arm and across her shoulder until his fingers were lying against the base of her neck. "I didn't realize things were that way in your home. But I'm sure you must still love them and they you. Maybe I could help you—go with you to speak with them," he offered.

Angela didn't know what was more disturbing, his touch or his words. "No!" she blurted loudly. Then realizing she'd made too much of a protest, she added more gently, "I mean, I'm just not ready to deal with my parents yet, Jubal. But thank you for trying to help."

More than restless now, Angela placed the remainder of her cake and coffee on the end table next to her, then left the couch to walk over to the fireplace.

As she stared pensively into the flames, Jubal came up behind her and curved his hands over the tops of her shoulders. Instinctively, her eyes closed, her heart began to hammer with anticipation.

"What are you doing way over here?" he murmured at the back of her neck. "Away from me?"

In spite of the heat, she shivered. "Wondering what I'm doing here—with you." Torn by the war inside of her, she turned and looked up at him. "I'm not sure our being together is wise."

"Angie—"

Shaking her head, she interrupted him, "Earlier this evening, Jubal, you talked about scraping off scabs, opening up old wounds. Well, that's what being with you does to me. I keep remembering—"

Before she could finish, his hands were drawing her against him. "Don't say that, Angie. Don't let the past keep us from finding happiness together. Let me show you how good it can be." The urgency in his voice matched the eager roaming of his hands against her back. "We can both leave the past in the past and move forward. Isn't that the most important thing now?"

Moving forward. Oh yes, how wonderful it would be if she could tell him the truth about Melanie and the three of them could become a family. But he'd violated her trust in the worst kind of way. Who was to say he wouldn't lull her into dreaming about happiness again, then leave her hanging out to dry just as he had five years ago?

No, he wouldn't do that now. Because he was a different man from that Jubal in the past, she rationalized. Geraldine and her whole family viewed him as a steady and reliable man. Angela had to see him in that way, too. Otherwise, she could never allow him to be a part of Melanie's life.

"I—want to believe you, Jubal. I'm just not sure I can."

Groaning with frustration, he pressed his cheek next to hers. "I'm asking for another chance, Angie. That's all. Just a chance to prove to you that we were meant to be together."

Feeling as though the floor was shifting beneath her feet, she grabbed hold of his upper arms and tilted her head back just enough to see him. His hands came up to gently frame her face and suddenly the touch of his fingers, the sensation of his hard body pressing against hers spun her senses to that place where only he could take her. Other than the crackling fire, there was nothing else in the room, in the world, but the two of them.

"Oh Angie," he whispered against her cheek. "Let me show you how much I want you—need you."

Maybe it was those last words that got her. Angela wasn't exactly sure what sent her resistance crumbling like a sand castle at high tide. All she knew was that she wanted to feel his lips on hers, his arms crushing her so close that nothing could come between them.

"Jubal. Jubal." His name whispered past her lips as she speared her fingers through his thick hair, drawing his face down to hers.

Pure need growled in his throat as his lips came down on hers in a blind rush of consummation. The tender assault had Angie gripping his shoulders, her lips parting, her lower body fitting itself against his.

Like a violent storm, hunger, need and love, all whipped together and plowed through every inch of her. Heat followed its path. A heat so scorching that it left her body trembling, her skin damp.

Kissing Angela was like putting one foot in the stirrup on a skittish bronc, Jubal thought. He didn't dare move too quickly to throw his leg over the saddle or she might bolt in a wild run. But restraint had never been one of his stronger traits and having her soft little body crushed against his was doing all kinds of things to his common sense.

Her lips tasted sweeter than the cake they'd just eaten and when her mouth opened, his tongue automatically pushed between her teeth to explore the dark, honeyed crevices inside. Against him, he could feel her body shudder ever so slightly, her fingers curl against his chest.

His own body was reacting like a randy teenager touching a female for the first time. Already his loins were aching to the point of exploding and the pain finally forced him to lift his mouth and whisper against her lips.

"Let me make love to you, Angie. Let us start over. Now. Tonight."

Her brown eyes swam with moisture as she looked up at him. Then a helpless groan sounded in her throat. "This isn't the way for us to—start over."

His hands gathered at the small of her back, anchored her hips to his. "Can you think of a better way?"

Shaking her head with surrender, she whispered, "I'm crazy. I'm crazy for wanting you like this. For giving you another chance to hurt me."

"But I'm not going to hurt you, Angie. Not ever again."

He could feel the last bit of her resistance dissolve as her body melted against his, her arms lifting up to circle his neck. Weak with triumph, he kissed her one last time, then took her by the hand and led her down a short hallway and into a small bedroom.

Just inside the door, he whispered, "Wait here."

Angela stood where she was, her whole body trembling with anticipation, her mind racing with uncertainty. Was she about to leap off a cliff, she wondered, or was starting over with Jubal her real destiny?

Across the room, Jubal switched on a small lamp and an oval of dim, golden light spread across the wooden floor and part of the bed. As he turned to face her, she started toward him. The few steps it required to reach him felt as though they were made on clouds and she was moving through a foggy dream.

She sensed, more than saw, the plainness of the room, the heavy wooden furniture, the soft thrum of raindrops pattering against the windowpanes. Her focus was on

Jubal, his face so softly serious, his outstretched hand beckoning her to his side.

"My darling."

It was all he said as he took her into his arms and began to kiss her all over again. The demanding search of his lips built a need inside her that she couldn't deny, nor hide, and she gave her mouth up to his in total abandonment.

The erotic connection was enough to take their breaths and force their hungry lips apart. As they stood looking at each other, tears stung Angela's eyes and she blinked them rapidly to hide the proof of her flooded emotions.

Pressing his forehead to hers, he said, "Tell me you want to be here, Angie. Tell me that you want to make love to me."

Reaching for the buttons on his shirt, she began to slide them apart. "I want to be here, Jubal. I want to make love to you."

Pushing the fabric aside, she leaned her head forward and pressed her lips to his hot skin. The moment she did, his hands were in her hair, pulling the shiny pins from the elegant twist. After the brown tresses fell to her shoulders, his fingers plowed through the silken mass, then moved to the hem of her sweater.

Soon, she was wearing nothing but black undergarments, strips of charming lace positioned to cover the most intimate parts of her body. Jubal slipped a finger beneath a bra strap and slid it downward toward one full breast.

"Sexy," he murmured with appreciation, his hands gliding over her skin like water.

Grunting with pleasure, he gripped both sides of her waist and tossed her gently back onto the bed, then quickly began to shed the rest of his clothing.

Once he joined her on the bed and pulled her into the tight

circle of his arms, the hard heat of his body pushed away all of Angela's fears and inhibitions. Nothing mattered now except that he wanted her and she wanted him.

With deft, urgent fingers, he opened the clasp of her bra. As soon as the lacy fabric was out of the way, his mouth sought out each nipple, teasing, tasting, licking until the twin peaks were hardened into rosy-brown buds.

Eagerly, need pushing her every movement, she arched her upper body toward his in an effort to get closer, to show him just how much she ached for him.

Splaying his hands against her back, he held her next to him and lifted his head just enough to see her face. The raw need that flickered in his eyes was more than she'd expected to see and she quivered in response.

"A few minutes ago I didn't think I could get inside you fast enough. But now—" His hands moved away from her back and began to slide over her breasts and across her belly. "Seeing you like this…I just want to touch every inch of you—to find out if you feel as good as I remember. And you do—oh yes, you do."

And he felt just as good to her, Angela thought, as she closed her eyes and let her senses drink in the sweetness of his hands roaming over her curves, heating her skin. This was the man she loved. The only man she would ever love. Had she always known that? Or had this very moment told her?

The questions were forgotten as she began to do some exploring of her own. Before long, the soft trail of her fingers against him had Jubal groaning with mindless want, pulling her beneath him and poising his hips over hers.

"This is kind of—late to be asking," he said, his jaw clenched with the battle to control his arousal, "but do I need to get protection?"

Suddenly she was remembering a long time ago, when the fire between them was so heated that contraceptives were sometimes forgotten. Melanie had been a result of that reckless behavior. But since he didn't know that, he could only be playing safe.

For one split second, the thought of her getting pregnant a second time with Jubal's child sent a tiny spurt of sanity through her brain, causing her to wonder if she was making a mistake. But the touch of his hands, the heat of his lower body pressed against hers was enough to dispel any doubts and she quickly reached up and pulled him down to her.

"There's no need. I'm protected with the pill," she whispered, then explained. "I take them for other health reasons."

With a satisfied grunt, he bent his head and captured her lips with his. She was opening her mouth, meeting the hungry search of his tongue, when his knee parted her thighs and he entered her with one smooth thrust.

The sudden connection shocked Angela's senses and sent a keening moan to the back of her throat.

Jubal momentarily lifted his head and she opened her eyes to see his face hovering over hers, his green eyes soft with concern.

"Are you okay?"

She would never be okay until she knew for certain that he was back in her life to stay. But that was a worry she wasn't about to dwell on now. Loving Jubal for this night had to be enough.

"Yes. Oh yes!"

A slow grin bent the corners of his lips and then he began to move inside her, slowly, temptingly, sending wave after wave of pleasure to rock her body.

Chapter Seven

Three days later, Jubal was telling himself he should be walking on a cloud. He'd made love to Angela. That should be enough to convince him that a future with her was more than just a hope, it was an actuality. Yet doubts continued to nag him so that he was desperate to see her again to make sure their time together had meant as much to her as it had to him. This evening, an emergency with a horse that had cut his foot badly on a piece of corrugated iron had kept him working late. Tendons had been involved in the injury and he'd spent the last hour carefully sewing everything back together.

"I think that just about does it, Pete." He carefully placed the sedated horse's hoof back onto the concrete floor, then turned to the young wrangler who was quickly becoming his best assistant. "Wrap him with gauze and then cover the whole bandage with duct tape."

The younger man tilted the brim of his hat back on his head as he looked skeptically at Jubal. "Duct tape? Isn't that for other things? Like a quick plumbin' fix or somethin'?"

Jubal chuckled and gave the wrangler a pat on the shoulder. "It's good for a lot of things. Including keeping bandages clean and protected from an animal's teeth." He glanced back at the dark gray horse. "After he wakes up take him out to a pen where he can graze. But tell the other wranglers not to put any other horses in there with him. He doesn't need any excitement until that foot begins to mend. And you might wait a few hours before offering him any grain. I expect he'll be off his feed until the anesthesia wears off anyway."

Pete nodded, then asked worriedly, "Will he be okay, Doc? I mean, he won't limp forever, will he? Gunsmoke is one of Matt's favorite geldings."

"He'll be fine," Jubal assured him. "Now you'd better get after that gauze before he wakes up."

"Sure thing, Doc. And I'm sure glad you're here now. Before you came we would've had to load Gunsmoke into a trailer and haul him all the way to Victoria to be treated. You being here saved him a lot of misery."

"Thank you, Pete. I'm glad I'm here, too."

The wrangler hurried away to take care of the bandaging and Gabe Trevino, the Sandbur's head horse trainer, stepped up to Jubal. For the past hour, the man had remained close by, as though Jubal had been working on one of his relatives rather than one of his horses.

"Pete's right, you know," Gabe said. "We're lucky to have you here on the ranch. Before you came, Matt and Lex and I were constantly having to patch up animals and carry them into Victoria to a vet."

"Just doing my job," Jubal told him.

"Well, that was a great job of surgery you just performed on Gunsmoke. A few months from now I doubt anyone will be able to tell he was injured."

Jubal especially appreciated the horseman's praise and he reached out and gave the man a gentle slap on the shoulder. "Thanks, Gabe. Coming from you that means a lot. And don't worry, I'll keep a close eye on him."

The two men talked for a few more minutes, before Gabe finally left the surgery unit. Jubal went to a small washroom to remove his dirty scrubs and rubber gloves. Once he was back in his jeans and shirt, he walked out to glance at Pete's progress with the bandage.

Satisfied that Gunsmoke was still doing well, Jubal exited the operating area and entered his office. The spacious room was floored with expensive tile, the walls textured and painted a cool green. A dark red couch and two armchairs were placed at one end, while the opposite end was filled with a large desk made of cherrywood. Nearby, another desk was equipped with a computer and the other technical devices needed to run a business.

It was late in the evening, and the winter sun had already fallen behind the oak trees standing outside the windows. Beyond the tree limbs, a yard light had flickered on to illuminate several stock pens. A north wind was kicking up dust and swirling bits of hay from a half-eaten round bale.

From this spot on the ranch yard, Jubal couldn't see the house where Angela lived, but he knew it wasn't far away. Just as she wasn't far away from his thoughts. In fact, since they'd made love three nights ago, he'd done nothing but think about her.

If he looked at things logically, he realized he should be

singing and dancing, shouting to the rafters. She'd made love to him in the most giving, trusting way he could have ever imagined. She'd clung to him as though she needed him, loved him, never wanted to let him go. Yet later, when the night was nearly over, he'd felt her withdrawing, pulling a curtain between them. And when he'd pressed her to set another date, she'd evaded making any sort of commitment to see him again. Why? Could she truly never forgive him for marrying Evette?

With a silent groan, he crossed over to the computer and switched off the hard drive. It was well past time to call it a day. But tonight he wasn't going straight home. He was going to Angela's. Even though she'd not invited him, he was going to invite himself. Because he couldn't bear to go another day without seeing her.

He was about to flip off the lights and leave the office when his cell phone rang. He pulled the instrument from his belt loop and stared in faint shock at the name illuminated in the small square.

What was his mother doing calling him? He hadn't spoken to her in months and even then their conversation had been cool and brief. His parents had never forgiven him for ending his marriage to Evette, or refusing to stay in Cuero under their controlling hands. Jubal didn't hate his parents. Far from it. He loved them. He just couldn't let them rule his life.

His features grim, he flipped open the phone. If something had happened to his father, Carl, he wanted to know about it.

"Hello, Mother."

"Have I caught you at a busy time, son?"

"I was just leaving my office," he admitted.

"Oh. You have an office now?"

Closing his eyes, he pinched the bridge of his nose.

First his parents had been disappointed in him for choosing to be a vet. His father, Carl, was a bank executive and they'd expected Jubal to follow in his footsteps. Then, seeing they couldn't fight him on his choice of profession, they'd done the next best thing and tried to control where and how he would build his veterinary practice. His leaving Cuero a few months ago had left his parents very bitter, but Jubal was beyond feeling guilty.

"It might be hard for you to believe, Mom, but this one is even nicer than the old one."

She cleared her throat and sniffed. "Well, that's difficult to imagine. But if you say so."

"I do," he quipped, then asked, "Is something wrong? Is Dad okay?"

"He's fine. He's working overtime at the bank tonight. I thought it would be a good time to call you—catch up on things and see what your plans are for Christmas."

Are you going to put up a Christmas tree? Angela's question suddenly raced through Jubal's head. When she'd talked about the holiday, she'd smiled and her eyes had actually glowed. She'd looked like the young Angie he'd fallen in love with and the sight had made him very happy.

"I'll be staying right here on the ranch."

Dinah Jamison let out a disapproving huff. "Oh, Jubal, why? You don't know those people. Not well enough to be spending Christmas with them. Don't you think it's time you came home and gave your parents a little attention? Carlotta is going to be here on Christmas Day. I know you'd enjoy seeing your sister."

Of course he would like to see Carlotta. His older sister had always been a loving sibling, understanding the difficult terms that Carl and Dinah had imposed on her brother.

She'd not condoned their behavior anymore than Jubal had, but she'd been more forgiving. Maybe because her female heart was a bit softer than his. Or perhaps she'd found it easier to overlook their faults, since she'd not been the one directly affected by their interfering ways.

"I'll see Carlotta soon. But I can't make any promises about showing up for Christmas. I have—other plans." Like finding the biggest blue spruce in Texas and inviting Angela and Melanie over to help him trim it.

"What plans could be more important than your parents?" she demanded.

Drawing in a bracing breath, he rested one hip on the corner of the cherrywood desk. "I've found, Angela, Mom."

There was a long pause and then she sputtered, "F-found? I didn't realize she'd been missing. Or that you were looking for that woman."

That woman. Back when Evette was making demands, doing her best to stick permanent claws into Jubal, his parents had sided with the mayor's daughter without even bothering to take the time to get to know Angela. The Malones were considered strange, religious zealots by most folks in the area and the Jamisons had quickly decided that a daughter from such a family was totally unsuitable for their son. A lying, conniving socialite had been more to their liking, he thought bitterly.

Anger rose in his throat like bitter bile, but he forced himself to swallow it down and be civil to his mother.

"For the past five years, I've unconsciously looked for Angie's face in every crowd, on every street."

"No wonder your marriage to Evette failed!" Dinah scolded. "You weren't even trying to forget that woman."

"Quit saying 'that woman,' Mother. Her name is Angela.

And my marriage to Evette failed because it never should have happened in the first place. Even Evette understood that much—especially after she lost the baby. A baby which was never mine in the first place. A fact you and Dad conveniently want to forget."

There was another long pause, then Dinah said in a choked voice, "Oh God, this is stupid, Jubal, to be rehashing all of this now. All that happened years ago!"

"Yeah, and it's still hurting me. Angela was crushed and now she doesn't want to trust me. But I'm trying like hell to rebuild our relationship."

Dinah gasped. "Rebuild! Why would you?"

Jubal raked a weary hand through his hair. "Because I love her. I've always loved her. So if you want to give me something for Christmas this year, just leave me alone. You couldn't give me anything better than that."

Dinah started to argue, but Jubal's patience had worn too thin to listen. He simply snapped the phone shut and terminated the harping voice on the other end of the line.

Across the ranch yard, Angela had just gotten home from a long day at the Sanchez house and was wearily trying to deal with Melanie's demands.

"But I wanta go now, Mommy! Can't we?"

"I'm sorry, sweetheart," Angela said, as she hung both their coats in the small hall closet. "It's too late to drive all the way to Victoria tonight. By the time we get there, Santa will already be in bed."

Melanie sniffed with disappointment. "But I gotta see him. I gotta tell him what I want."

Turning away from the closet, Angela stroked a pacifying hand over her daughter's head. "It's still a long time before Christmas, honey. You'll have plenty of time to talk to Santa before then."

Scrubbing her eyes with two little fists, Melanie tried to dry her tears. "Marti says I have to tell Santa early or I won't get what I want."

Taking her daughter by the arm, Angela led her back into the living room and sat her down on the couch.

"Mel, Santa is watching you right now and he isn't happy when he sees little girls crying." Easing down beside her daughter, she wiped at the tears streaming down Melanie's flushed cheeks. "Now what is it that you need to tell Santa about?"

Clamping her lips together, Melanie shook her head. "I can't tell you. I have to tell Santa Claus."

Sighing, Angela studied her daughter's troubled face. "It must be very important to you."

Melanie's mouth popped open. "It is—"

The child's words were suddenly cut off as a knock sounded, making both of them look with surprise at the door.

"That's probably Santa right now," Angela said as she got up and hurried over to answer the second knock. "He must have come to see why you're crying."

Melanie jumped up from the couch to race after her mother's heels. "I'm not cryin' now, Mommy. See?"

Angela's hand paused on the doorknob as she took a second to glance down at Melanie. The child had made an attempt to wipe her eyes and plaster a fake smile on her face.

"That's better. Much better," Angela told her as she tried to hide her own amused smile. "Now step back and we'll see who's at the door."

"Peek through the window first, Mommy, remember? It might not be Santa."

"Thank you for reminding me," she told the child as she stood on tiptoe and glimpsed out the small square of glass.

The sight of Jubal standing on the porch shouldn't have surprised her. After all, the man lived and worked right on this very property. Yet, she'd not heard from him since their time together three nights ago and she was beginning to think his ardor for her had cooled, that he'd decided the two of them couldn't recapture what they'd once shared.

Hurriedly, she opened the door to greet him. "Jubal," she said with a happy rush. "Come in."

With his hands thrust in the pockets of his jacket and a faint grin on his face, he stepped over the threshold, then waited for her to shut the door behind him.

"Sorry for just showing up without an invitation," he said. "I seem to be doing that often, don't I?"

"Twice," Angela agreed. "But I'm not counting."

His gaze landed on her face and she suddenly felt very self-conscious. Which was ridiculous. The man had seen her with nothing on and in the most vulnerable way a man could see a woman.

"Are you…am I interrupting anything important?"

Smiling faintly, Angela pointed down to Melanie, who was glued to her side. "Not really. Just trying to reason with a whiny daughter."

Pulling off his cowboy hat, he hung it on a peg by the door, then turned his attention to Melanie. "Hello, young lady. Are you having a problem tonight?"

With one finger stuck in the corner of her mouth, Melanie nodded up at him. "Mommy won't take me to talk to Santa. Now I'm gonna miss gettin' the gift I want."

"Who says?"

"Marti. He says I have to talk to Santa real early—a long time before Christmas. And Mommy won't take me to town. That's where Santa is right now."

"And you think Marti knows what he's talking about?"

Melanie gave him a huge nod. "He's twelve now. He knows everything."

"I'll just bet he does." He slanted an amused look over to Angela before glancing back down to Melanie. "Well, I wouldn't get all worried just yet. One year I didn't get to talk to Santa at all and I still got what I wanted."

Melanie's green eyes flew wide. "You did? How?"

"I wrote him a letter."

Melanie wrinkled her nose. "But I don't know how to write."

Folding his arms against his chest, he glanced suggestively at Angela. "I'm sure your mother can do that chore for you."

Thrilled at this idea, Melanie instantly began to jump up and down and tug on her mother's hand. "Will you, Mommy? Please, write the letter for me!"

"Whoa!" Angela instructed. "We have a guest. Besides that, it's time for supper."

Melanie looked crestfallen and Jubal quickly squatted on his boot heels to be on her level.

"You know what?" Jubal consoled her. "I'll bet if you ask your mother nicely, she'll write the letter for you after supper. Wanta try?"

Eagerly falling in with his suggestion, Melanie flung her arms around her mother's waist and squeezed tightly. "Will you write the letter after supper, Mommy? Please? I'm askin' real nice."

Angela looked over her daughter's head to Jubal and gave him a conspiring wink as she patted Melanie's shoulders.

"I promise I'll write the letter," she assured the girl. "Now run and wash up while I put supper on the table."

The girl skipped out of the room and Angela shot Jubal a grateful look. "Thanks for suggesting the letter. Now she won't go to bed tonight worrying about her Santa list."

He shrugged. "Sometimes kids listen to an outsider before they do a parent."

An outsider. Dear God, how awful that sounded, she thought guiltily. He was also Melanie's parent. A part of Angela wanted to scream out the truth. But she tempered the urge. She was just starting to get back into Jubal's life again. The threads between them were still far too fragile to wham him with that sort of news right now. Besides, while she couldn't deny that she was falling for him again, she was still wary of trusting him, especially with Melanie's heart. Angela knew what it was like to be rejected by her father. She never wanted that to happen to Melanie.

"I suppose," she said, then quickly changing the subject, she gestured toward an open doorway that led to the kitchen. "Would you like to join me in the kitchen while I fix our meal?"

"I'd like that."

He followed her into the small kitchen, taking off his jacket and hanging it on the back of an oak dining chair, while at the cabinet counter Angela began to pull several containers of already cooked food from a brown paper grocery sack.

"I have to admit that I'm cheating tonight. Cook prepared chili today and since there was plenty left over, I couldn't resist." She glanced over her shoulder at him. "Will you join us? Or have you already eaten?"

Crossing the short space between them, he settled close

to her side and she was suddenly swamped with the urge to slip her arms around him, to have him hold her close.

"I haven't eaten. I just finished up a bit of surgery on a horse a few minutes ago. I thought—I wanted to come by and see you before I went home." Reaching out, he gently touched the back of her hair. "You haven't called."

Her hands paused on the lid of one of the plastic containers. He was so close she could feel the heat of his body, smell his unique masculine scent. Memories of him kissing her, stroking her naked body paraded through her mind, making her stomach clench and her throat tighten.

"You haven't called, either," she pointed out gently.

His fingers meshed more deeply in her hair, reminding her how very much she'd missed him these past three days.

"The other night," he said softly, "when I brought you home, I got the feeling that you didn't want me to push you for another date."

Angela dared not glance up at him. Just resting her eyes on his dear, familiar face was enough to make her want to fling herself against his chest and sob out how much she loved him. But she couldn't do that now. Not when there were still too many secrets and unanswered questions between them.

"I'm sorry if I gave you that impression. I guess the whole evening—us being together—had left me a little shocked."

"Then you *do* want me to push you?"

The teasing note in his voice lightened the awkward tension between them and she chuckled softly. "That wasn't exactly what I meant. But I have missed you. Actually, I was beginning to think you must have regretted the other night."

The words were hardly out of her mouth before he was

pulling her into his arms, burying his face in the side of her neck. Groaning with relief, Angela wrapped her arms around his waist and held on tightly. It was terrible how much she needed this man, how much her happiness depended on him.

"I don't regret one moment, darling," he murmured. "Do you?"

Her throat aching, she managed to push out one word. "No."

Nuzzling her hair aside with his nose, he pressed his lips to the exposed curve of her shoulder. "I've been afraid, Angela. When I told you good-night you seemed so—withdrawn. Tell me that everything is all right, honey. That we're going forward—together."

Swallowing away the lump in her throat, she carefully eased from his light embrace and turned to the food containers. She'd not been withdrawn, she thought miserably, she'd been downright worried. If Jubal was really serious about the two of them having a future together, how was he going to feel when he discovered she'd kept Melanie's birth a secret from him? The truth might tear them apart forever.

You should have told him when you first discovered you were pregnant, Angie. Then none of this would be happening now.

The little voice inside her was right, she thought, dismally. But Angela hadn't discovered she was pregnant with Melanie until nearly two months after she and Jubal had broken up. By then he was already married to Evette. And Angela hadn't wanted to break up a marriage. Especially when the wife was pregnant.

But you were pregnant, too, Angie. You needed Jubal, too. And Melanie needed a father.

Shoving those agonizing thoughts aside, she tried to flash Jubal a teasing smile. "Everything is okay, Jubal. We're going to have a meal together. What more could you possibly want?"

Chuckling, he bent his head and placed a lingering kiss on her cheek. "I can think of an endless number of things. But since your daughter is awake—they'll all have to wait."

Your daughter. She's your daughter, too, my love. Everywhere Angela looked, everything she said and did brought the reality home to her.

Actually, she was slightly surprised that Jubal hadn't noticed that Melanie's green eyes were the image of his, that he'd not put her age and the timing of their affair together. Apparently he thought she'd jumped into bed with another man right after they'd parted. It wasn't an image she wanted him to have of her, but she realized the truth of the situation was probably going to hit him much harder.

As if on cue, Melanie suddenly skipped into the room. Angela was shocked to see that the girl had changed from her jeans and sweater to a dress that Angela normally saved for her to wear to Sunday school.

Instinctively she opened her mouth to order Melanie back to her bedroom to change again, but just as quickly she stopped herself. Melanie was obviously dressing up for Jubal's sake and Angela wasn't about to embarrass her daughter for wanting to impress the man.

"Wow!" Jubal exclaimed as he turned his attention to Melanie. "Is this the same little girl that was crying earlier? It can't be. This little girl is much too beautiful to be her."

Giggling, Melanie twirled around on one toe and Angela was surprised to see that she hadn't pulled on her ballet slippers. Instead she was wearing her red cowboy boots with the white fringe around the tops.

"It's me," Melanie proudly announced. "And I'm just as pretty as Mommy. Sometimes."

Laughing, Jubal gave Angela a sidelong wink. "You certainly are."

Almost an hour later, the chili and cornbread was eaten. At the table, Jubal was finishing a last bite of cherry pie and a cup of coffee while Angela dealt with the dirty dishes.

Melanie waited obediently in her chair until her mother had finished cleaning, then gathered a pencil and notebook from a cabinet drawer.

"Here we go," Angela said as she took a seat next to her daughter and to the left of Jubal. After carefully writing the date on the right hand corner of the paper, she looked to Melanie. "Okay, sweetie, tell me what you want me to say and I'll write it down exactly like that. Dear Santa—"

Having her belly full of food had put a sleepy fog to Melanie's eyes and she blinked them rapidly as she struggled to remain awake.

"I've been a very good girl this year. My mommy says so—most of the time." She paused long enough for Angela to finish writing the block print. "I used to want lots of gifts for Christmas. But it's not nice to be selfish. So I just want one gift this year. A pony. With brown and white spots and a long tail. I want to name him King and for him to be my very own."

Even though Angela was flabbergasted over this request, she continued to painstakingly print out the rest of the message. Across from her, Jubal smiled with appreciation.

"What about a saddle, Miss Beauty Queen? Don't you think you'll need one of those to ride King?"

Careful to keep her face hidden from Melanie, Angela shot Jubal a silent, bewildered plea to keep his suggestions to himself.

Smiling coyly, he held his palms upward in an innocent gesture. "What? I'm just trying to be helpful."

"Sure you are," Angela said dryly.

"Yeah! Yeah!" Melanie exclaimed. "Put a saddle on the list, too, Mommy. A black one with shiny stuff on it! Reckon Santa will bring that, too?"

Angela bit back a sigh. Here she'd been thinking how much better Melanie's Christmas was going to be now that she had a job with a significant salary. But she'd not planned on her daughter coming up with anything like this. Melanie was going to be greatly let down on Christmas Day. Still, maybe it would be a lesson for the girl. She needed to learn that she couldn't always have what she wanted or asked for. It was a lesson that Angela had certainly learned.

"Honey, are you sure you wouldn't rather have a baby doll? Or maybe a new bicycle with training wheels? You're getting big enough for one of those."

Melanie's brown curls swooped across her little face as she shook her head emphatically back and forth. "No. I want a pony. I want King."

Jubal's hand reached over and closed around Angela's forearm. She looked at him cautiously.

"This is her Christmas list," he reasoned. "She should be able to tell Santa her most fervent wish. If you want her to dream, then let her dream big."

"But Jubal, a pony—" Angela began only to have him pull the note and pencil from beneath her hand.

"A black saddle with shiny silver conchos," Jubal spoke

as he scratched the words onto the notebook. "And a black bridle with pistol bits," he added for good measure, then tore off the sheet of paper and carefully folded it. "Better get an envelope for this, Mom. We need to mail it off first thing in the morning."

A few minutes later, Melanie climbed into bed with the letter safely tucked beneath her pillow. Jubal watched from the doorway as Angela kissed the little girl good-night, then turn out the overhead light.

Once they were back in the living room, he said, "She's quite a girl. She must fill up your life in so many ways."

Angela sank onto the couch, then lifted the cat to the floor in order to make room for Jubal to join her. "It never gets too quiet around here," she joked, then her smile quickly faded. "Raising her alone is not always easy."

"Looks to me like you're doing a great job."

She could hardly agree, but one thing she did know, the job would have been much easier if he'd been around. If she'd told him about Melanie, would he have chosen to be a father to her? At the time Angela found out she was pregnant, they had both believed he'd fathered Evette's child. By the time Melanie was born, she was long gone from Cuero and no one, especially her parents, had bothered to tell her that Jubal had gotten divorced. Oh Lord, how tangled and torn, how miserably unfair it had all been.

Pushing her dark musings aside, she said, "I was really looking forward to buying Melanie some nice gifts this year for Christmas. Up until this year, I've hardly had a dime to spare. But now—with this pony thing going on with her—I don't know what I'm going to do. I guess I'll just let it be a learning experience to her that we don't always get what we wish for."

As Jubal's gaze gently roamed her face, a wry smile twisted his lips. "Angie, you want your daughter to believe in Santa and yet you're unwilling to believe in miracles yourself."

She studied him from the corner of her eye. "What do you mean by that?"

He reached over and touched his fingertips to her cheek. Angela found herself leaning closer, needing his affection as much as she needed air to breathe.

"Have you ever stopped to think that maybe Melanie will get what she's asked for?" he asked.

Angela playfully rolled her eyes. "Sure, Jubal. On Christmas morning, I'll look outside and see a brown and white pony standing on the lawn."

"Stranger things have happened. Just look at the two of us. I thought you'd probably married and left Texas. Our being together again is a miracle."

Were they really together again, Angela wondered. Or was she a fool for thinking they could ever mend the wounds and scars between them?

Lowering her eyelids to hide the shadow of doubt in her gaze, she murmured, "I'm not sure I believe in miracles, Jubal."

Suddenly his forefinger was beneath her chin, tilting it upward. Angela's eyes fluttered open just in time to see his mouth descending toward hers.

"That's something I'm going to do my best to change," he promised.

Chapter Eight

Two days later, Angela entered the Cattle Call Café in downtown Goliad and took a seat in the back. For more than two years, she'd worked at the country style restaurant as a waitress. The wages had been minimal, but thankfully the tips had been generous enough to allow her to pay the rent and the most pressing college bills, and keep food on the table for her and Melanie.

The long, rectangular room had a high ceiling and a Formica-topped bar that spanned one end. Round wooden tables and chairs filled the remaining space and during the week, the place was usually packed with diners. Most of them were working townsfolk, local ranchers and lawmen.

Today, Angela was doing the weekly shopping for the Saddler house and had taken the opportunity to call Nicolette and her sister, Mercedes, and invite them to lunch. Unfortunately, Mercedes was accompanying her husband, Gabe, on a horse buying trip and was unable to accept the invitation. As for Nicci, it wasn't often that the physician's assistant could get away from the clinic, but today she was only working a half day. Angela was grateful to the woman for making time for her. She desperately needed to talk to a friend.

As Angela sipped on a cup of coffee, her mind lingered on Jubal's visit two nights before. The kisses he'd given her had stirred her, left her aching and wishing that every night of her life could be spent in his arms. But doubts continued to nag her. Especially at the thought of explaining Melanie to him.

"Hey, is this my chair?"

Angela looked up to see Nicolette standing next to the table. Behind her stood her cousin Matt's wife, Juliet Sanchez. Since the tall blonde had been Angela's friend even longer than Nicci, she was doubly excited to see both women.

"Nicci! You've brought Juliet with you! How wonderful!"

Rising from the chair, she kissed each woman on the cheek, then quickly gestured for them to join her at the table. "I haven't ordered yet," she confessed. "Are either of you really going to eat or will you just pick at a salad?"

"Angie, you know me," Juliet said with a laugh. "Cheeseburgers and fries. They make the best ones here."

Juliet was a reporter for the *Fannin Review,* the local weekly newspaper, and most of her lunch hours had been spent here at the Cattle Call, until she'd married Matt and given birth to little Jess. Now she'd cut down her work to only three days a week. And the same went for Nicolette, since she'd married Ridge and given birth to Sara Rose a few months ago.

"Good," Angela told her, "because I'm hungry."

The three women took seats around the table and after

a waitress wrote down their orders, Angela's grateful gaze encompassed both friends. "Thanks for coming today. We see each other in passing at the ranch, but it seems like we never get a chance to really talk that much."

Nicci chuckled. "How could we? We're always dealing with crying babies."

Juliet smiled at Angela. "Melanie getting excited about Christmas?"

Angela sighed. "She's already made a list."

"You don't sound too pleased about that," Nicci commented with a laugh.

Shrugging helplessly, Angela said, "She wants a paint pony. A real one."

Both women chuckled as though Angela was worrying over nothing. But then they would, she thought. Getting ponies for their children would be as easy as lifting the phone and placing an order for a pizza.

"Well, that's expected," Nicci said. "She sees the horses on the ranch. And Marti and Gracia are always riding. She wants to be like them." The pretty brunette waved her hand in a dismissive way. "I'm sure we can come up with something suitable for her to ride."

"I'll tell Matt tonight," Juliet added. "With more than two hundred horses in the Sandbur remuda, I'm sure he can come up with a spotted pony."

Angela wasn't about to accept a horse from the ranch for Melanie's gift. But she wasn't going to argue that point now. She had far greater worries on her mind.

Her finger running absently around the rim of her coffee cup, she said, "That's very generous of you both, but Melanie's outlandish Christmas wish isn't what I wanted to talk to y'all about."

Spotting the serious look on Angela's face, Juliet scooted to the edge of her seat. "You want to have a real talk? Gee, I thought we were just going to eat and gab. Is something wrong?"

Frowning with concern, Nicci quickly added, "Angie, if anything is bothering you, you understand that Mother will do everything in her power to fix it. We want you to be comfortable and happy on the ranch."

Leaning back in her chair, Angela quickly shook her head. "I love my job. And I'm so grateful to both of you for helping me like you have. Raising Melanie alone has been scary sometimes. Being on the ranch has made things much better for us."

Nicci held her palms up in an inviting gesture. "Then what's going on? Frankly, you look a bit peaked. There are shadows under your eyes."

Angela unconsciously touched a forefinger to her cheekbone. "I'm not sick. I just haven't been sleeping all that well."

Nicci shot her a look of disapproval. "Why haven't you come to me before now? I can prescribe something safe for you that will help you rest at night."

"It's not a sleeping problem," Angela argued.

"You just told us it was," Juliet put in with a worried frown.

Angela groaned. She'd never talked to either woman about Melanie's father. And the two women had been considerate enough to never ask. Cook had figured it out on her own, but the older woman kept personal secrets close to her chest. Angela was certain that Cook hadn't breathed a word to anyone about her connection to Jubal.

"All right," Angela said before she could swallow down the words, "I'll just come out with it. Jubal is the problem. My problem."

Both women appeared completely blank.

"Jubal?"

"The vet?"

The women blurted the two questions at the same time. Angela answered both of them with one grim nod.

"Jubal and I—" she paused, cleared her throat, then tried again. "We knew each other before—back in Cuero."

Juliet and Nicci exchanged curious glances, but before either of them could fling more questions at Angela, the waitress returned with their lunch orders.

After the young woman placed the plates of burgers, fries and tall glasses of sweet iced tea around the table, she made sure the women were content with their food, then hurried away.

Angela stared after her with empathy. "I'll bet her legs are killing her, poor thing. It's not easy working here during the lunch rush. You barely get a moment to breathe."

Juliet reached over and patted Angela's hand. "Those days are over for you. You'll be getting your teaching degree soon. That should be enough to put a smile on your face."

"Not when there's a man involved," Nicci put in flatly, then looked at Angela and asked, "Okay, what is this about Jubal? Are you trying to tell us that he's an old flame or something?"

"Or something." Angela shook salt and pepper on her burger, then took a bite.

Across the table both women were leaning forward, waiting expectantly for her to go on. Unable to face her friends, Angela stared at the burger she was gripping with both hands.

"What is this 'something'?" Juliet prompted. "Did you have a thing for the man and now it's uncomfortable to have him working nearby?"

Glancing up, Angela forced the words past her tight throat. "I had more than a thing for Jubal. I had—his baby."

To say that Nicci and Juliet were stunned would be an understatement. Completely flabbergasted, they both stared at her as though she'd morphed into someone else.

"Baby," Nicci was the first to echo softly. "You mean Melanie? Jubal is her father?"

Relieved that the truth was finally out, Angela nodded. "We had a relationship that lasted nearly four months. Melanie was a result of our time together."

"Oh my Lord," Juliet said with a groan.

"Does he know?" Nicci asked.

Closing her eyes, Angela passed a hand over her forehead, wishing she could wipe away the mental pain.

"I'm afraid not."

Juliet gasped.

Nicci sat in dazed silence.

"It sounds awful even to my own ears," Angela went on. "But I had my reasons."

Juliet was the first to respond to Angela's stunning declaration. "Maybe you should tell us about those reasons."

Angela pointed to the plates sitting in front of her friends. "Your food is getting cold. I'll explain while we eat."

"Well," Nicci said as she picked up her burger, "you've certainly knocked the wind out of me. I didn't have a clue that you knew Jubal. And apparently he hasn't mentioned it to anyone on the ranch. I've not heard a whisper. Have you, Juliet?"

The blonde shook her head. "No. The only thing Matt has told me is that Jubal used to live in Cuero and that he's single with no family. Is that true, Angie?"

Angela nodded. "Jubal is divorced."

Nicci's eyes widened with insight. "Was he married while the two of you were together?"

Knowing that Nicci's heart had once been ravaged by a cheating husband, she quickly put her friend's fears to rest. "No. Jubal was a single man when I first met him. He'd been casually dating another woman off and on, but he'd assured me that it was totally over with Evette. She was the mayor's daughter and after a while Jubal decided she was a little too spoiled for his taste."

"So what happened?" Juliet asked.

Angela drew in a bracing breath and began, "I fell in love. Completely. And it seemed like Jubal loved me, too. We even started to plan a future together. But then Evette began calling Jubal, begging him to come back to her. When he refused, she shocked him with the news that she was pregnant. She said that if he didn't come back to her, she would do harm to herself."

Nicci gasped with outrage. "So she was threatening to harm his child, too? What kind of woman would do such a thing?"

"A desperate one, I suppose," Angie answered miserably. "Jubal didn't want anything to happen to the baby and, frankly, I could understand his feeling that way. I just wanted him to deal with Evette in some other way, force her to seek therapy or something. Instead, he decided he needed to be a father to the child and the best way to do that would be to marry Evette. When he told me his decision, we abruptly ended our relationship and never spoke again. A couple of months later, I realized I was pregnant, but by then Jubal was already married and I saw no reason to cause more problems. After all, Evette had already used a baby to wedge herself into his life. I had no intentions of doing the same thing. I wanted him without snares, with nothing but love between us. That didn't happen."

Juliet muttered a few curse words under her breath while Nicci simply shook her head in dismay.

"Is that why you moved away from Cuero?" Nicci asked.

Angela grimaced as she forced herself to swallow down a bite of food. Only minutes earlier she'd felt famished, now the food felt like stones in her stomach. "Partly. You see, I'd just turned twenty and was still living at home while going to college—or at least trying to. We didn't have much money at the time, so I was working my way through classes. But my parents were horrified when they learned I was pregnant. They banished me from home and told me not to return until I became a 'decent' married woman. They didn't want me around, ruining their righteous reputation. And Jubal—well, I didn't want to see him married to someone else, so I moved to Goliad."

"So you came here homeless, pregnant and alone," Juliet stated incredulously. "With no man or family to help you."

Nodding, Angela was surprised to feel the sting of tears at the back of her eyes. She'd long ago stopped feeling sorry for herself. It was Melanie, and the idea of her having no family around her, that got to Angela more than anything.

"I can't imagine anything more horrible," Nicci said as she picked up her tea glass.

Juliet slanted a look at the woman. "Oh yes, you can. What about a husband who lied to you for nine years, who had you believing that something was wrong with you when you couldn't get pregnant when all along he'd had a secret vasectomy? Men. They can be real bastards."

Angela frowned at the woman's display of disgust. "But

Juliet, why do you sound so cynical? You're wildly in love with your husband."

The blonde's features glowed at the mention of her soul mate. "I love Matt madly. He's wonderful. But I suffered through some real stinkers before I met him."

Sighing, Angela said, "Well, I don't think of Jubal as a bastard. He was trying to do what he thought was the right thing. I—this probably isn't going to make sense to either of you, but I—still love him."

Leveling a concerned gaze on her, Nicci asked, "And what about Jubal? Have you talked to him since he's come to the ranch?"

Angela mentally groaned. If talk was the only thing she'd done with Jubal, then she might not be sitting here agonizing over her next step. As it was, she'd jumped straight into the fire without any sight of the future. Now she was looking for a cool patch of sanity.

Feeling a hot blush rush to her cheeks, she answered, "Uh—yes. We've talked and he told me that shortly after he and Evette married she miscarried. And then, I guess out of guilt or something, she confessed to Jubal that the baby hadn't been his."

"Not his!" Juliet whispered with shock. "You've got to be kidding!"

Angela shook her head. "Seems Evette had been having an affair with a married businessman in Victoria. When the man refused to get a divorce and marry her, she decided to use Jubal as a means to save her social image."

"If that was the case, then why didn't Jubal try to find you after the divorce?" Nicci questioned.

"That's what I've been asking myself. He says he figured I'd already found someone else. And that I was too young for him anyway. But I'm wondering if it was because he simply didn't love me enough to come looking for me."

"Maybe," Juliet muttered. "But the guy had been put through the wringer by a deceitful woman. Just think about it. He married her in good faith, believing he was going to be a father. Not only is the child lost, but he learns the baby wasn't his to begin with. Believe me, that would do something to a man's trust, his emotions. Could be he wasn't ready to go looking for any woman—until now."

Nicci frowned at her cousin-in-law. "I can't believe you're being so understanding toward the man."

Juliet rolled her eyes. "Look, all I'm saying is that it was a bad situation for everybody concerned. And Angela hasn't exactly helped matters by keeping Melanie a secret from Jubal."

Nicci turned a regretful look on Angela. "Juliet's right. Don't you think it's time you finally told him?"

Jabbing her fork into a crisp French fry, Angela grimaced. "Yes. But I'm afraid. Melanie believes her father has simply chosen to live far away from us. What if she gets close to him and then things don't work out? She'd be devastated."

"Melanie needs to have a father," Nicci reasoned. "Even if he isn't around on a day-to-day basis."

Juliet cast Angela an empathetic look. "I understand. You're wondering if you can trust him to stick around for the long haul."

Leaning back in her chair, Angela glanced around the busy cafe, but all she could see was Melanie on the couch, cuddled next to Jubal as he read her a story, Jubal at the kitchen table writing Melanie's wish list. Her daughter did need to know her father. But how was she ever going to find the courage to tell him?

A troubled frown marking her brow, Angela mumbled, "That's part of it."

Reaching across the table, Nicci placed her hand gently over Angela's. "Just remember, Juliet and I will always be here for you."

By the time the weekend rolled around, Jubal had called her with plans to take her and Melanie out shopping for a Christmas tree. Since Melanie would be joining them, Angela knew she wouldn't have a chance to have the talk with him about his daughter, and a part of her was relieved.

For years, she hadn't dwelt much on the fact that Jubal was unaware of Melanie's existence. After all, she'd believed he was living happily with his own wife and child. Seeing him that night at the Saddlers' party had knocked her for a loop, and since then the truth about their daughter had been eating at her like an unstoppable disease.

If she was going to continue to spend time with the man, she had to be totally honest with him. Otherwise, their relationship would be meaningless. Still, another day or two would give her more time to prepare, and to find the courage to finally tell him that over four years ago, she'd given birth to his baby.

Late Saturday afternoon, Melanie stood lookout for more than an hour before she finally spotted Jubal's truck pulling into the drive.

"He's here, Mommy!" The child yelled excitedly. "Come on! Let's go!"

Hurrying from the bedroom, Angela picked up her handbag and the booster seat for Melanie, then sprinted after her daughter as the little girl bounded down the front steps and ran to meet Jubal.

The waning sunlight was beginning to dip, leaving a nip to the north wind. The cooling temperature had given Angela an excuse to wear her coat which was still pinned with the little rhinestone horse.

Jubal grinned with open appreciation as she joined him at the truck. "Two beautiful girls for company. A guy can't ask for more than that."

And a girl couldn't ask for a sexier man than the one standing before her, Angela concluded. This evening he was wearing a chocolate brown leather jacket over a dark burgundy shirt and blue jeans. A black cowboy hat was slanted low on his forehead, shading the gleam in his green eyes. Just looking at him melted every bone in her body.

"Wait until we take you on a huge shopping round before you say that," Angela teased.

Laughing, Jubal took the booster seat from Angela and fastened it to the back seat of the truck. After he lifted Melanie inside, he carefully strapped her in and reminded her not to climb out while they were traveling.

"You look like you've done that a thousand times," Angela commented as he shut the back door and turned to her. "You must have practiced on your sister's children."

"No. Carlotta doesn't have any children. She got a divorce last year."

"Oh. I'm sorry to hear that," she said a bit awkwardly. "I guess—well, some of us just got off on a bad foot."

Shrugging, his gaze gently wandered over her face. Then he smiled, as though looking at her cured everything.

"She's doing okay," he said quietly. "And so are we—now."

Clouds of worry suddenly shaded her heart. He believed everything between them was okay. *Oh God, please let it always be okay*, she silently prayed.

Struggling with a smile, she said, "I'm beginning to think that we both ended up here on the Sandbur for a reason."

Touching a hand to her face, his head bent enough to place a swift kiss on her lips. The brief touch was so intimate, so sweet that she wanted to stand there and cling to him, but the spell was broken when he opened the door and reached for her forearm.

"So you *are* beginning to believe in miracles," he said as he helped her into the truck.

"I'm working on it," she conceded.

"Good."

Once she was settled in the seat, their gazes locked and the intensity she saw in his green eyes shook her. She was uncomfortably reminded that no matter how much she loved him, there was a high, wide wall standing between them, one that he didn't even know about. What would happen once it came tumbling down?

She made up her mind to push that question out of her thoughts this evening. They couldn't have the discussion tonight, with Melanie there. And besides, Christmas was coming. It was a time to be joyful.

"Let's go, Jubal! I'm hungry!"

Melanie's impatient calls from the back seat broke the moment between them.

"Sounds like someone is getting antsy," he said with an amused chuckle, then shut the door and hurried around to the driver's seat. "We're on our way, little princess."

Once they reached Victoria, Jubal allowed Melanie to choose what the three of them would eat. After a noisy meal at a fast food restaurant, they drove to a nearby discount store where Jubal purchased the tallest blue spruce he could find, along with a shopping cart full of decorations to trim it with.

As the three of them maneuvered through aisles thick with holiday shoppers, Jubal spoke to Melanie, who was riding in the front of the shopping cart. "I have a sneaky suspicion that Santa is in this store somewhere. Would you like to see him?"

The child cocked her head to one side as she contemplated Jubal's question. "Well, he has my letter. Ya think I need to?"

Clearly amused, he glanced questioningly at Angela. "What do you think, Mommy? Should she remind the old fella about the pony?"

"Jubal!" Angela scolded for his ear only. "There are other things she can put on her wish list."

"Yeah." Jubal grinned. "Like a bridle and saddle."

Knowing she was fighting a losing battle, Angela groaned in surrender. "Okay. Let's go look for Santa."

They found the jolly, red-suited man at the front of the store, sitting in a throne-like chair. A line had formed up to the roped-off area that separated him from the traffic of shoppers. At the moment a boy around five years old, dressed in jeans and a football jersey, was sitting on Santa's knee reciting a list of toys long enough to choke an elephant. Near the back of the line, where the three of them were waiting, a little girl was screaming at the top of her lungs and trying her best to tear away from her mother's firm grip.

"I don't wanta see that old man!" she yelled at her mother. "I wanta go home!"

"Aimee, don't argue!" the flustered woman scolded. "You have to see Santa in order for me to get a picture. And we have to have a picture to send to your grandparents. Now behave!"

Bending his head close to Angela's ear, Jubal muttered, "Great reason for the kid to see Santa. Cheap gifts for the grandparents."

If the situation hadn't been so estranged with her own parents, Angela could have laughed at his comment. As it was, she simply asked, "Are you sure you want to go through this? We could be in line for a long time."

He chuckled. "Angie, when you deal with fractious animals all day long, a screaming kid is pretty mild. Besides, this is the first time in many years that I'm seeing all the things that go on during the Christmas holiday."

"And what were you doing during those years?" she asked curiously.

"Running the clinic. It's the same for animals as it is for humans. Accidents and illnesses don't recognize holidays."

"You're still a doctor this year," she pointed out.

"Yes," he agreed, "But being the Sandbur's resident vet has taken away a lot of the extra work involved in running a public clinic. Now I actually have a bit of leisure time—to spend with you and Melanie," he added with a sly grin.

At that moment, Angela felt downright awful. Melanie was one of the reasons she'd not even attempted to date. Most men didn't want a child tagging along, being in the way, putting a cramp on things. But Jubal appeared to be exactly the opposite. He seemed to actually care about Melanie and enjoy her company.

Oh, if only she could turn back the clock, Angela thought wistfully. If only she could change the choices she'd made so long ago. Regardless of the situation with Evette, Angela should have told Jubal that she was pregnant, too. It had been his right to know and she'd taken it away. In some ways, she'd behaved even worse than he and she seriously doubted the regret she was now feeling would ever go away.

"Angie, is something wrong?"

Glancing up, she saw him frowning down at her and realized that her anguished thoughts must have shown on her face.

Quickly, she placed a reassuring hand on his arm. "No. I was just thinking how nice this is of you to take time to deal with Mel."

In spite of the busy crowd around them, his eyes slid sensually over her face. "Why wouldn't I?" he asked. "She's as sweet as her mother."

He'd hardly gotten the words past his lips when Melanie began to tug on Jubal's arm. Looking down, he could see that child had become uneasy.

"Is something wrong, pumpkin?"

She glanced skeptically at the man sitting on the elaborate throne. "I don't wanta talk to Santa. He looks scary. I wanta leave."

Bending close, Jubal patted Melanie's cheek. "He might look scary," he told the child, "but he's really nice. When your turn comes to talk to him, you want me to come along with you?"

"Oh yes! That would make everything good," she exclaimed, then as a measure of gratitude, she flung her arms around Jubal's neck and kissed his cheek.

Rising back up to his full height, Jubal sheepishly rubbed the kissed spot on his cheek as he glanced once more at Angela.

"I think I've just been properly charmed," he said.

And she'd fallen in love all over again, Angela thought. Now she could only wonder about the future. Maybe she and Jubal could throw away the broken pieces of their past and start anew. But Melanie was a part of those pieces. The child would be a constant reminder between them.

Jubal had asked Angela to forgive him. But once he found out about his daughter's existence, would he be able to forgive Angela? Dear God, she wished she knew.

Chapter Nine

Later that night at Jubal's house, Angela and Melanie watched as Jubal trimmed the huge tree with a hand saw, then secured it in a stand at the opposite end of the room from the fireplace.

While Jubal, with the help of Melanie's coaxing chatter, loaded the fragrant limbs with tiny, colored lights, Angela went to the kitchen to make hot chocolate.

By the time their cups were nearing empty, the tree was completely adorned with garland, ornaments and candy canes.

"Well, there's only one thing left to do," Jubal declared as they all stood back to study their handiwork. "We need to get the angel up to the tippy top. I wonder who might do the job?"

"You! You, Jubal! You're big!" Melanie exclaimed.

Jubal walked over to the last of the ornaments and pulled

the angel from its box. Back at the discount store, he'd allowed Angela's daughter to choose the angel she liked the best. Melanie had surprised him by picking a plain, Raggedy Ann type figure with yarn for hair and simple wings made out of cotton sheeting rather than gossamer. Apparently the child already realized that the shiniest one wasn't always the best. He admired Angela for teaching her such things.

"Oh, I can't reach that high," Jubal told the girl. "I'm gonna need some help. Wanta help me?"

Melanie nodded and he scooped her up in his arms, handing her the angel. "Okay. When I lift you up, you sit her on the top of the tree. Think you can do that?"

"Yeah! Lift me, Jubal! Lift me!"

Behind them, Angela watched father and daughter finish the tree trimming, wishing for a camera to capture the image. For all she knew, this might be the only time the three of them would be spending an evening like this together. But then, she wouldn't need a photo to remember these moments, she realized. The specialness of them would always be stamped into her memory.

A half hour later, with the tree twinkling in the background and holiday music playing on the stereo, Angela and Jubal sat close together in front of the fireplace. Melanie lay nearby on a braided rug, coloring with the crayons and coloring book Jubal had purchased for her at the discount store.

"I can hear the wind howling outside," Angela murmured drowsily. She snuggled her head on Jubal's shoulder and breathed in his sultry, masculine scent. "But it's as warm as toast in here. You're very lucky to have a fireplace. Where do you get the wood?"

"Some of the cowboys have been clearing a few north

pastures where the mesquite has grown thick. Since they have to haul it away, they offered me all I wanted."

"Lucky again," she murmured.

The arm draped along the back of her shoulders shifted until his hand was resting against the side of her upper arm. As his fingers slid softly against her skin, he said in a low voice, "*Lucky* is having you here next to me."

A wry smile tilted her lips. "That's a cheesy line if I ever heard one, Jubal Jamison."

His other hand moved beneath her chin and lifted her face up to his. "Maybe I do sound corny, but that's the only way I know how to say it, Angie. While we were apart, I dreamed about being with you like this, and I hated myself for letting things come between us."

Once his remark would have caused her to tear into him with accusations, to remind him that their future had been wrecked because of Evette and his choice to abandon her for the woman. But now she was beginning to realize that she didn't have any right to read him the riot act. Not when her own behavior had been less than blameless.

"Thinking of you with Evette was never easy," she quietly admitted. "There were times that I think I actually hated you."

He released a rueful groan. "And now?"

Now she loved him. It was a simple fact. "Now I—I'm trying to trust you again."

His forefinger traced a path across her cheek until it was touching her lips. "Oh, Angie. One of these days you're going to realize you can trust me. I'm going to spend the rest of my life proving it to you."

He bent his head to kiss her, then suddenly remembering Melanie's presence, he glanced to where the child was lying on the rug. Her cheek was now resting against the pages of the coloring book, her eyes closed.

"She's asleep," he declared with a bit of surprise. "It's still early. Is that normal?"

"So much excitement has worn her down," Angie reasoned. Easing from his light embrace, she rose to her feet. "I'd better get her off the floor before the draft gives her a cold."

Jubal followed her up. "I'll carry her to one of the bedrooms so she'll be comfortable," he said.

A few minutes later, Melanie was curled up in the middle of a double bed, safely tucked beneath a heavy comforter.

Standing beside the bed, Jubal affectionately touched a finger to the child's brown curls. "I think she had a good time this evening. She even seemed to enjoy talking to Santa."

"Only because you were there to keep her safe," Angela pointed out, then with a hand on his arm, she gestured for the two of them to leave the room.

Once the two of them were out in the hallway, Jubal asked, "How long will she sleep?"

"If we don't disturb her, probably all night. Why?"

Snaring an arm around her waist, he pulled her out of the bedroom doorway and into the circle of his arms.

"Because I want to make love to you," he whispered in her ear. "Having you in my bed again is all I've been able to think about."

Shuddering with undisguised longing, she tilted her face up to his. "Jubal, we can't. Not with Mel in the house with us."

Frowning, he rested his forehead against hers. "And what do married couples do? Forget about sex because their children are living in the same house?"

"No. They go into the bedroom and shut the door."

A wicked grin slanted his lips. "That's exactly what I was thinking we should do."

Before she could make any sort of response to that, he grabbed her hand and quickly led her down a short hallway to the room where they'd made love a week ago.

Compared to the living room, the space was cool, and except for a slither of moonlight slanting through the windows, filled with deep shadows. Even so, they had no trouble finding each other in the darkness. Angela groaned with need as his mouth fastened roughly over hers. His hands skimmed urgently down her sides, then cupped the flare of her bottom.

"Do you know what it's been like for me this week? You—this—has been burning a hole in my mind."

His hoarse voice whispered against the side of her neck and warmed the blood that was already racing like molten lava through her veins.

"It's been—the same—for me," she said between tiny gasps of pleasure. "And I—shouldn't be wanting you like this, Jubal. But I do. Oh, I do."

Her confession fueled his desire even more and, spearing his hands into her hair, he cradled the back of her head, while his mouth feasted on her soft lips, his tongue plunged inside to mate with hers.

In a few short moments, the room was reeling around them and Jubal's body was crying out to feel her warm skin, to have her naked and writhing beneath him. While his lips supped and nipped at hers, his hands reached to pull the thin sweater she was wearing over her head.

She lifted her arms and he tossed the garment to a far-off corner of the room. Then without pause, he did away with the rest of her clothing and quickly shed his. When he was finally finished, he circled her waist with his hands and lifted her back onto the bed.

Before he followed her down, he leaned over and switched on the lamp on the nightstand. The soft pool of light painted her pale face and dark brown hair, her rose tipped breasts, the hollow of her belly and her smooth thighs. For long moments, he studied the beautiful picture she made with her hair fanned around her head, her eyes glittering with the invitation for him to move closer, to touch and kiss.

"Did you need a light to find me on this big bed of yours?" she teased.

With a low, sexy chuckle he stretched out beside her and skimmed his hand over her ribs, across the side of her waist and onto the curve of her hip. "Hardly. But seeing you like this—" He dipped his head and circled one nipple with his hot mouth, rolled it between his tongue and teeth, then lifted his head to look at her. "Doubles the pleasure. You're the most beautiful thing I've ever seen, Angie. These years without you, I was hollow."

She closed her eyes and he could see her throat working as she struggled to swallow. The sight of her trying to deal with such heavy emotions stabbed him right in the heart. All he wanted to do was draw her close, love her, never let her go.

"Me, too, Jubal."

Her whispered admission touched him, filled him with the desperate need to comfort her, to protect her fragile heart.

Bringing his face next to hers, he rubbed his lips over her forehead, pressed tiny kisses along her cheeks, then poised his lips over hers.

"That's all over with now, my darling. We're together now. And that's the way it's going to stay."

The choked moan in her throat called to him and he kissed her until he could feel her body going pliant, her arms slipping around his neck and clinging to his back. By then, his manhood was engorged and aching, but the need to linger, to explore every sweet pleasure her body had to offer prevented him from making the ultimate connection. Because he knew once he entered her, once her delicious warmth wrapped around him, he would be quickly lost.

With one smooth motion, he rolled to his back and pulled her along with him until she was draped over him, her breasts flattened against his chest, her hips pressed against his lower abdomen, her smooth legs tangled with his.

His hands pushed her long hair away from her face. Then, with his gaze locked on hers, he eased her upper body back until she was straddling him and the intimate folds between her thighs were teasing, sliding against his erection, bringing his blood to a boiling point and sending a sweet, fiery pain straight to his loins.

Above him, Angela was hungry to touch him, to run her hands over the wide breadth of his shoulders and chest, down his corded arms. To kiss his damp salty skin and allow her tongue to tease his flat male nipples.

Loving Jubal, touching him gave her pleasures that could not be compared, but mostly it filled her heart with love. A love so deep that she had to fight to keep the tears from sliding down her cheeks.

Lifting her head, she gazed at him through a watery wall of emotions. "We're not dreaming anymore, Jubal." Lifting her hips, she brought herself down on him, absorbing his hard arousal within her wet, velvety home. "This is—real. Sooo—real."

She began to move against him and he cried out with an intensity that shattered her composure and urged her to quicken her movements, to draw from him the very thing she needed the most. His love.

Somewhere along the way, he once again shifted their positions so that Angela was lying beneath his hard body, her legs wrapped around his hips. By then, their movements had reached a frenzied urgency and as he plunged into her over and over, her body, her every nerve, tautened to the breaking point, her breaths turned to harsh rasps against her throat.

Climbing, reaching, straining. Her lungs were on fire and just as she thought she was going to collapse from the wild exertion, she felt herself slipping to a place where there was nothing but intense pleasure ripping through her, washing wave after wave of exquisite sensations through her body.

Somewhere along the way, she could hear Jubal's guttural cry, feel the grip of his hands on her buttocks as his warm seed poured into her. And then slowly, slowly she began to drift back to earth, back to his sheltering arms.

After a few moments, she became aware of her cheek pressed beneath his shoulder, the damp, warm weight of his torso draped limply across her.

Weak and satiated, she lifted a hand to his head and pushed her fingers into his hair.

"I know I'm crushing you," he murmured. "But I don't want to move. Can we stay here like this forever?"

A tired smile curved Angela's lips. "We might have to eventually get up and find some sort of nourishment."

"Yeah, I guess so," he said with a good-natured groan. He rolled off her and onto his side, then immediately pulled her into the curve of his body. As she settled next to him, he added, "I suppose Melanie will want breakfast in the morning. I'll cook you both something special."

Her cheek was pillowed on his arm and she took pleasure in breathing in the musky scent of his skin. "You know how to cook?"

His chuckle caused his chest to move against her back. "Out of necessity. I've always considered it easier to give an angry tomcat his rabies shot than to cook. But I can fry meat and potatoes."

"And that's enough to keep a man happy," she said with a grunt of amusement.

His hand slid to her breast and cupped its weight in the palm. "Among other things," he whispered languidly.

Shocked that desire was already stirring once again, she closed her eyes and drank in the dreamy pleasure of his touch. "Breakfast sounds nice, but Mel and I can't stay here all night, Jubal."

"Why?"

Clearly perplexed by his assumption, she turned to face him. "Why? Because I don't want Mel to wake up and find us in bed together. That may sound as though I'm raising my daughter in an old-fashioned way, but that's just the way I am. I guess more of my strict upbringing wore off on me than I thought."

"Hmm," he purred against against her cheek. "You might not believe this, but I actually feel the same way. So you can sleep with Melanie while I sleep in here."

One of her brows arched upward. "Really?"

Grinning, he slid his mouth across her cheek, then down

to her lips. "Now don't go thinking I'm all gentleman, my darling. Because I don't expect to let you out of this room for a long while yet."

Chapter Ten

Three days later, Angela was in the kitchen of the big ranch house, helping Cook make a batch of pecan pralines when the telephone hanging at one end of the cabinet rang.

Muttering a word of impatience, Cook put down her wooden spoon and went to answer it.

"Keep stirrin' that, honey," she flung over her shoulder at Angela. "We don't want the sugar to scorch."

"I will."

Angela had picked up the spoon to do the older woman's bidding when suddenly Cook called to her again.

"The call is for you. I think you'll want to take it."

Cook left the receiver lying on the cabinet and went back to tending the pralines. Angela hurried to take the call, all the while expecting it to be Geraldine with more instructions about the party for the coming weekend. It would be the first of many Christmas parties to be held on the

Sandbur, and the matriarch was counting on Angela to see that all the decorations for the house were done well in advance, not to mention the pounds of candy that she and Cook were preparing ahead of time.

"Hello. This is Angie," she spoke into the receiver.

"Angie," Jubal said, "sorry to interrupt your work. I wanted to let you know that something has come up. I can't make it to your house tonight."

Jubal's unexpected message sent her spirits plummeting. For the past few days, since their tree-trimming weekend, she'd planned to meet with him as soon as she could find a free night and a babysitter for Melanie. Hiding from him that he was Melanie's father was gnawing at her to the point where she was hardly getting any sleep at night.

"Oh. I'm sorry about that." She nervously pushed a hand through her tumbled hair, then lowered her voice. "I was really planning on seeing you tonight."

"I've been dreaming about it all day," he admitted. "But Lex wants me to go with him to look over a herd of crossbreds he's thinking about buying. The cattle are up at Seguin and we won't be back until late. Maybe we can make it tomorrow night."

Her mind raced ahead. Another sleepless night of worry wouldn't kill her, just put a few more dark circles under her eyes.

"I understand, Jubal," she said, not bothering to hide the disappointment edging her voice. "I'll call you tomorrow afternoon and we'll go from there. Okay?"

"I'll be waiting, honey," he said softly. "Until then, think of me."

She swallowed as a ball of anguish lodged in her throat. "I am," she whispered. Fearing she was going to get teary eyed if he said any more, she quickly ended the call. "Good-bye, Jubal. And have a safe trip."

Trying her best not to appear deflated, she hung up the telephone and rejoined Cook at the gas range. Peering into the pot of boiling ingredients, she observed, "Looks like it's almost ready to pour up. Maybe you'd better check it with a thermometer."

Cook snorted. "I ain't never used one of those things in my life. Why would I start now?"

"To make the job easier?"

"Hmmp. What could be easier than just looking at it? Or dripping a drop into a cup of water?" Shaking her head with dismay, she said, "You young folks are all alike. You want gadgets to do all the work for you."

"That's because we haven't learned everything yet," Angela reasoned with her.

"Hmm, well, I'm beginning to see that for myself." Cook glanced pointedly at Angela. "Looks to me like you're falling hook, line and sinker again for the doc man."

Sighing, Angela reached up in the cabinet and brought down a roll of wax paper. "You think that's a bad thing?"

Cook continued to stir the boiling sugar. "I didn't at first. But the more you're around the man—the worse you look."

Grimacing, Angela ripped off a long piece of the wax paper and spread it over the cabinet counter. "I'm worried, Cook. I haven't been sleeping."

"That's just the point," Cook shot back. "If the man was making you so happy, you'd be sleeping like a log. A smile would be on that pretty face of yours instead of worry lines."

"It's more complicated than just loving the man, Cook." Sighing, she turned to face the woman. "I'm sure you've already figured out his part in Melanie's birth."

Cook gave her one affirmative nod. "I guessed."

Another long sigh slipped past Angela's lips. "Jubal doesn't know. He thinks someone else fathered her after we broke up."

The woman studied her for a moment, then turned her gaze back on the cooking candy. Even so, Angela could see she was cogitating the whole messy matter.

"Guess you had a good reason not to tell him," she said after a bit.

"Yeah. He married someone else."

Cook glanced her way. "He obviously ain't married now."

"No."

Reaching to the front of the stove, Cook switched off the flame. "Well, honey, all I can tell you is that it's not good for a woman to be alone. I've been that way for nigh on forty-five years. It's not good for a man to be childless, either. I know about that, too. And from what I can see, a little girl deserves to have her father around."

"That's what I've been thinking." She returned the roll of wax paper to the cabinet shelf. "I'm just not sure how Jubal is going to feel about Melanie."

"If he's half the man Geraldine says he is, then he'll love her."

Yeah, Angela thought, he'd probably love his daughter no matter what. But once he learned the truth, would he love Angela?

The next afternoon, Jubal and Lex were riding horseback to a far west pasture. A herd of bulls hadn't been checked on in several weeks, and Lex thought it would be a good idea if Jubal rode along, just in case any of the animals needed medical treatment.

"Damn, I'd forgotten just how far out it is here," Lex said after the two of them had ridden about forty minutes. "I'll bet you wish you'd come up with an excuse to stay at the ranch yard."

"Not at all," Jubal told the other man. "The weather is beautiful. And I like any reason to ride. It's been so long since I've been on my own horse, he'll probably throw me sky high the next time I saddle him."

Lex laughed. "Bring him over to the ranch yard whenever you do. The wranglers always enjoy a little rodeo."

Jubal chuckled with him. "I'll get around to riding Biscuit over the holidays—when the ranch is a little quieter."

"Sorry, Jubal, I hate to tell you this, but the ranch never gets quiet." Lex looked up at the blue sky and sighed with pleasure. "Guess that's why I've always loved this place. Something is always happening, growing, changing. Keeps it all interesting." He glanced over at Jubal. "'Course, that's not to say that you won't get time off to spend with your family. You going up to Cuero for Christmas to see your folks?"

Jubal's strained relationship with his parents was something he didn't like discussing. But Lex was becoming a good friend and he didn't want to appear to be secretive or evasive. Especially when the whole Sandbur family had embraced him with open arms.

"I'm not planning on it. They'll be having lots of business people in for parties. That's not my thing."

Lex let out a good-natured groan. "Well, surely they couldn't have more parties than Mother. Shindig should have been her middle name. She loves to entertain."

"Geraldine is very good at it. And she does it from her heart—to give people an opportunity to have a good time."

Unlike Dinah and Carl Jamison, he thought grimly. Their main objective was to show just how much better off they were than the regular townsfolk.

"Yeah, Mom's a giver." Lex glanced across the rough land, his expression pensive. "I only wish Dad were still alive. He loved the holidays. He loved life in general." Shrugging with wry acceptance, he looked over to Jubal. "It's been eleven years since he died, but I still miss him like it was eleven days. Don't judge your parents too harshly, Jubal. One of these days you might not have them around."

Lex was right, Jubal thought. He should be making an effort to forgive his parents. After all, the only thing they were guilty of was wanting what they thought was best for him. And parents all over the world committed that sin everyday. He should have never let his frustration toward them simmer so long. But somehow, losing Angela had seemed doubly worse with his parents praising Evette at every turn. Still, he was the one who'd let Angie go. And now that he'd found her again, it was time to let go of old resentments.

"You're right, Lex. I'll make it a point to contact them."

Thirty minutes later, the two men spotted the Brahman bulls. Fortunately, all of them appeared to be healthy, except for one who was carrying less weight than he should have been.

Jubal dosed him with medication to kill parasites, then drew a tube of blood to take back to the ranch for testing.

"In a couple of weeks, he should be looking better," Jubal said to Lex. "The blood will tell me if there's anything serious going on. But I'm betting not."

Lex replied, "Matt and I would like to turn the herd of heifers we bought last night onto this bunch of bulls. What do you think?"

Jubal nodded. "Sounds good. But can you hold off a few days? I want to make sure none of them have shipping fever." He patted the bull on the shoulder as though he were a dog. "Old blue here might get really sick if he's exposed to that."

"You know best, doc. That's what we have you for. A few days it is," Lex agreed.

The men walked away from the herd of grazing bulls and back to the mesquite tree where they'd left their horses tethered. The day was warm enough to be out without a jacket and the sunshine bearing down and heating Jubal's shoulders made his thoughts leap to spring. By then, he wanted Angela to be his wife. He wanted the three of them to be in his home as a family. The mere idea filled him with hope. Something he'd been missing for the past five years.

As the two men mounted up and headed back to the ranch, Lex sang a bawdy song under his breath while Jubal thought about the evening ahead and seeing Angela again.

"Hey, Jubal, why don't you come to the house for supper tonight?" Lex suddenly invited. "Matt and Gabe are coming over to talk about sending a few foundation-bred colts up to Cane's Landing. Cordero thinks there's a good market in Louisiana for working ranch horses."

Pulling his mind back to his saddle partner, Jubal glanced at him. "So your cousin doesn't plan on coming back to the Sandbur any time soon?"

Lex shook his head. "Doesn't look like it. His father-in-law owns a good deal of property in Louisiana. He wants Cordero to use it, so we've decided to extend the Sandbur's horse division to another state. Cordero seems to like it there. But then he should," he added with a suggestive chuckle. "The man has a gorgeous wife and young son. I wouldn't be surprised to hear that Anne-Marie is expecting again. He has plans to raise as many kids as he does horses."

Jubal grunted with amusement. "Anne-Marie might have something to say about that."

Lex laughed. "Are you kidding? She adores Cordero. She'll give him anything he wants. Damn it, if I only had his charm, I might get somewhere with the ladies." He shot a speculative glance at Jubal. "By the way, some of the hands tell me they've seen you visiting Miss Angela's house. You work fast, buster."

Jubal felt his cheeks redden, which was ridiculous. Being romantically linked to Angela didn't embarrass him. He'd just not realized that the other men had noticed his comings and goings on the ranch. "Not really. We—uh, we knew each other before—in Cuero."

"Damn, Jubal. She looks a mite younger than you."

Jubal tried not to wince. His friends and acquaintances back in Cuero had never understood his relationship with Angela. In addition to the distance in their ages, she was from odd stock, the sort of people that others gossiped about when they lacked juicier news. Most everyone had thought he'd come to his senses when he'd married Evette. How little they'd known, he thought ruefully.

"She was almost twenty when we dated before."

"That daughter of hers is as cute as a button. Punch me if I'm getting too out of line, but did you have anything to do with that?"

Jubal absently popped the ends of his reins against the swells of the saddle. From the first night he'd met Melanie, his mind had been tormented with what-ifs. What if he'd fathered Melanie? How wonderful it would feel to hear that darling child call him daddy. But wishful thoughts couldn't change the facts, he thought dismally. "No. That happened after we broke up."

"Oh. Well, that's too bad. It would've been sorta nice if she'd been your daughter. That is, if you've got serious intentions toward Angie."

Before Jubal could make any sort of response to that, Lex laughingly shook his head and twisted around in the saddle so that he was facing him.

"Sorry again, Jubal. I know I'm butting in where I don't belong. But you see, when Angie came to work for us we—that is, all the family just sorta fell in love with her. She was like a little bird with a broken wing. We all wanted to fix things for her. And we wouldn't want her to get hurt. Not for any reason."

Any other man would probably have taken offense to Lex's subtle warning. Perhaps even been jealous of the good-looking rancher. But Jubal couldn't be. In fact, he was glad that Lex and his family loved Angela and wanted to make sure she was happy. She deserved a better life than the one she'd had before coming to the Sandbur.

"I'm ashamed to admit that I caused Angela some terrible misery in the past," Jubal admitted. "But that will never happen again. I promise you that, Lex."

The other man grinned. "Maybe you'd better make that promise to her instead of me."

"I plan to. I'm going to see her tonight."

"Oh. Guess that means you won't be over for supper."

This time Jubal was the one with the wide grin. "Nope. I've got a better offer tonight."

* * *

Angela didn't know why she was bothering to take extra care with her appearance tonight. She and Jubal wouldn't be leaving the house. No one would see her except him.

That's just it, silly. He's the one you want to look good for.

With that little voice mocking inside her head, she leaned closer to the mirror. The light makeup she'd added to her eyes and lips was soft and warm and thankfully added some life to her otherwise pale face.

After pulling on a thin red sweater, a denim circle skirt and a pair of black cowboy boots, she hurried out to the kitchen to put the last touches to the table.

She was folding a pair of linen napkins that Cook had insisted she borrow from the Saddler kitchen when she heard Jubal's strong knock on the front door.

Her heart hammering, she smoothed a hand over her hair and hurried out to greet him.

The moment he stepped over the threshold and she shut the door behind him, he pulled her into his arms and kissed her soundly on the lips. He smelled of cold wind and musky cologne and tasted even better than she remembered.

The kiss momentarily dazed her and she figured she looked a little drunk as she gave him a lopsided grin. "How did you know Mel wasn't here?"

He chuckled sexily. "I didn't. I just figured she needs to get used to seeing me kiss her mommy."

"Oh, so it's that way," she said playfully.

His eyes glided tenderly over her face. "Yeah," he said softly. "It's that way." He looked past her shoulder. "Where is the little angel, anyway?"

She cleared her throat as nervousness threatened to overtake her. *Everything will be okay, Angela. The man will understand that you couldn't tell him about Melanie. How could he not understand? He'd been married to another woman! A woman who'd also been pregnant!*

"Well—uh—I wanted us to be alone this evening, so Juliet graciously invited Mel to spend the night with Jess."

"Hmmm." He rubbed his cool cheek against hers. "I hope this time alone means what I think it does."

Heat rushed to her cheeks and colored them a rosy pink. Obviously his mind was on taking her to bed. But she couldn't allow that to happen until she'd talked with him. Otherwise, talk of any kind would be shoved to another day. And too many days without the truth had already passed. She only wished she'd come to that realization long before now.

"Well—sorta," she replied. "I mean, there's something I wanted to discuss with you."

That caught his attention and she watched his brows inch cautiously upward.

"You look serious," he said. "Is anything wrong?"

Trying to relax, she attempted to smile. "No. Nothing is wrong. It's just that I need to talk, that's all. Would you rather eat first? I have supper ready. Beef tips and rice."

One of his favorite meals. Any other time, Jubal would be grabbing her hand and heading straight toward the kitchen. But this news about a talk had knocked him off kilter. When a woman wanted to talk, something was usually wrong, even if she insisted it wasn't.

"I think I'd rather have the talk first," he answered.

Even though there was a faint smile on her lips, he could see her eyes blink nervously, her throat work as she swallowed. Had something happened since the last time he'd seen her to upset her? He couldn't think of anything.

Her small hand wrapped around his and Jubal allowed her to lead him over to the couch.

"Let me take your coat and hat," she said.

While he took a seat, she carried his things over to a nearby desk. When she returned and sank down next to him, he noticed that the poinsettia was still on the coffee table and the horse pin adorned the shoulder of her sweater. The sight of his gifts was a small measure of reassurance.

"Okay, what—"

"There's something—"

Their words tangled, making it impossible to understand what either of them had said.

Laughing softly, Jubal gestured graciously toward her. "You go first, my lady."

She looked away from him, but not before Jubal saw her biting down on her lower lip. In spite of her worried expression, her beauty grabbed him and he realized that the more time he spent with this woman, the more he needed her, loved her. She was filling up the empty holes in him and for the first time in years, he was beginning to feel truly happy again.

"I—uh—well, I actually don't know where to start," she murmured. "I've thought about this for days and I still don't know how to do it, Jubal."

"Angie, you sound so—torn. Has something happened? Something with your family?"

Her head bowed. "No," she said soberly. "This is about you and me. About what happened back when—when you decided to marry Evette."

Throwing a hand against his forehead, Jubal groaned loudly. "Oh God, Angie, do we have to get into all that again? I thought we were going to forget the past and move forward."

Her brown eyes sad, she looked at him. "I'm sorry,

Jubal. But this has to be said. Otherwise—well, I can't put our past behind us."

Jubal's gaze dropped to her lap. Her fingers were twisting and torturing each other in a fight to the death. Her obvious anguish filled him with apprehension and he wondered if he'd been fooling himself into thinking she cared as deeply for him as he did for her. Maybe this whole thing had just been physical to her. But he didn't want to think that. No. He couldn't think that.

Reaching over, he clasped her hands and gently smoothed her fingers flat against his. "All right, Angie. If it's that important, I want to hear it."

Her head lifted and his heart winced as he watched her lips tremble. He didn't want her to worry, to hurt or fear. He wanted to make everything right for her. As Lex had said, she'd been a bird with a broken wing. He'd caused that injury and he wanted to spend the rest of his life making up for the misery she'd gone through.

Long moments passed and when she still didn't speak, he touched fingertips to her cheek. "It's all right, darling. Tell me."

She closed her eyes and her fingers tightened around his. "Okay. It's about Melanie—about me getting pregnant. I—"

"That doesn't matter, Angie," he swiftly interrupted. "I don't care that you had an affair with another man. He and Evette are forgotten. Our lives are starting over—with each other."

The moan that sounded in her throat was the same sound he'd heard from the many wounded animals he'd tended. It said she was in pain and didn't know where to turn or whom to trust.

"You don't understand, Jubal. I—I didn't have an affair with another man. There's only been you. Only you."

For a moment, the significance of her words didn't hit him. Like a stallion proud of the mare trotting at his side, he was thrilled at the idea that she belonged solely to him. And then like an electrical wire brushing across his skin, the meaning hit him, jolted him to stunned disbelief.

"What are you saying, Angie? That...that Melanie is—that I'm her father?"

The one brief nod she gave him was like a fist whamming him in the face. The unexpected pain literally knocked him backwards and caused him to release his hold on her hand.

"That's—exactly what I'm trying to say," she said. "What I've been wanting to say for a long time now."

His mind reeling with a myriad of questions, he stared at her and tried to catch his breath. Melanie. Sweet little Melanie with her heart-shaped face and laughing green eyes! His daughter! Why hadn't he seen it for himself? How could he not have known?

"You've been wanting to tell me for a long time? Angie, we've been apart for five years! Melanie is—what? Four and a half? When was this time to tell me ever going to come? What if I hadn't come here to the Sandbur? What if we'd never seen each other again? Was I never going to know that I had a daughter?"

With each question he spoke, his throat grew so choked he could hardly speak. She'd crushed him right to the center of his being and like one of his wounded animals, he wanted to lash out.

"I—I don't know, Jubal," she answered miserably. "Up until I saw you a few nights ago at the party, I believed you were married to Evette. That the two of you were raising your child together."

Blowing out a rough breath, he rose from the couch and began to move blindly around the room. Only this afternoon he'd told Lex that someone else had fathered Melanie. God, how stupid that made him look, feel. And yet his heart was singing that he and Angela had a child together. A daughter!

"Leave Evette out of this," he finally managed to say. "This is about you—and the fact that you had my child without letting me know! That I've missed her birth, her baby years—I've missed—" He turned away from her and raked a trembling hand through his hair. "Oh God, I've missed so much," he whispered in a tortured voice.

"And what do you think I've missed, Jubal?"

The quietly spoken question had him spinning around, staring at her blankly. "I—I don't know. You've had Melanie all these years. I haven't."

Frustration propelled her off the couch and caused her to march over to within inches of him.

"Okay, you don't know, so I'll tell you. I missed having a husband to help me through those months when my body was weary and begging for rest. But I couldn't rest. I had to work, to shelter myself and my coming baby. I missed having a husband at my side at the hospital while labor pains tore me inside out. And later, well, later I can't begin to tell you all the things I missed because you weren't with me. Because you believed marrying Evette and fathering her child was the best thing for you!"

Chapter Eleven

By the time Angela spoke the last word, tears were streaming down her face. Poisonous, bitter tears that had been stored inside her heart so long that only a storm could release them.

"That decision has haunted me for years," Jubal said with a rueful groan. "I shouldn't have allowed anything or anyone to sway me away from you. I shouldn't have believed Evette. I shouldn't have had sex with her in the first place. I shouldn't have done a lot of damn things. But you shouldn't have kept your pregnancy from me, either. Didn't you think I would want to know? That I would understand?"

Her head dropped, then swung back and forth. "I wasn't exactly an experienced woman back then, Jubal. God knows you told me plenty of times that I was too young for you."

"You were. And it's my fault that I let our relationship

turn into something serious. But—" He paused and drew in a long, ragged breath. "If I'd known you were pregnant—that you'd had my child—things would have been very different."

Lifting her head, she stared miserably at him. "How so? You would have gotten a divorce and come to me? Do you think I would've been happy with that on my conscience? Tearing up a family, all the while knowing that I was your second choice? Think about it, Jubal! I was young and naive then, but I was certainly old enough to understand that I didn't want you under those terms."

Wiping the back of her forearm against her cheeks, she turned and walked out of the room.

Jubal was right on her heels as she entered the kitchen. "Okay, so maybe things were in a mess," he conceded. "But none of that changes the fact that I'm the father of your baby. That I had a right to know about her."

Gripping the edge of the kitchen table with both hands, she forced herself to face him. "Looking back, I can see that I made a terrible mistake by not going to you and telling you that I was carrying your child. But at the time I discovered I was pregnant, you were already married and I was so hurt I couldn't see straight. I think…maybe in a way, I wanted to keep Melanie from you—as a way to get back at you for hurting me. For choosing Evette and her child over me. Now I can see how selfish I was and I'm—terribly sorry."

His face taut, he walked over to her and wrapped a hand around her upper arm. With his free hand, he pulled out one of the chairs, then helped her into it.

"Look, Angie, this whole thing—it's not easy for me. I've already tried to live with one woman who lied and kept things from me. Now I've found out that you've been dishonest with me, too."

A rueful grimace tightened the corners of her lips. "I'm trying to explain why I did what I did."

"Well, frankly, there are still lots of things you haven't told me. Like why you're estranged from your parents. Does it have something to do with Melanie?"

"Only everything," Angela said with a weary sigh. "The minute they learned I was carrying your child, they called me the lowest names they could think of and kicked me out of the house."

For a moment she saw the rigid line of his jaw soften as though he understood some of the trauma she'd gone through after they'd parted. But then he turned away from her and the stiff line of his back, the clenched hands at his sides, assured her that he was still finding it difficult to come to terms with her shocking news.

"I recall your parents were very narrow-minded. Still, it's hard for me to imagine that they pushed you out of their lives. Was it because of me? Because I had done the dirty deed of fathering your child?"

Angela shook her head. "No. In fact, up until I became pregnant, they liked you. But then—well, I became a social disgrace to them. I guess they thought if they refused to take care of me, then you would. In fact, Dad was planning to confront you about making a decent woman of me. But then he learned about your wedding and that changed everything."

She looked at him skeptically while wondering what he could possibly be thinking. So far he'd not mentioned that he actually cared about Melanie or wanted to be her father. And that was the whole crux of the matter now, she told herself. It didn't matter how he felt about Angela.

Melanie's happiness and well-being came before everything else.

"What about you? Can you accept that you have a daughter with me?"

His gaze jerked toward hers and she could see a thousand haunting questions swirling in the depths of his green eyes. His pain cut into her, reminding her that she'd not been the only one to suffer these past few years.

"Obviously, you haven't told her about me," he said tightly. "That I'm her father."

Angela gazed at his stony face and wished for yesterday, before lies and mistakes ever wedged their way into their lives, to the time when his arms would already be circling around her, his lips inviting her to make slow, sweet love to him.

"No. She believes her father lives far away."

He moaned. "Didn't she ever want to know why her father wasn't around like other children's?"

Angela passed trembling fingers across her aching forehead. "Sometimes, she would ask. But I think just knowing that she had one out there somewhere was enough to satisfy her. After all, she grew up without a man in the house. She doesn't really understand the concept of having a daddy."

His eyes darkened but whether it was from anger or regret, she couldn't tell. His face had become a mask, a stiff replica of the warm, affectionate man who'd walked through the door only minutes earlier.

"And is that what you wanted for her?" he quietly demanded. "A life without a father?"

Her palm itched to reach up and slap his face. There was no question that she'd made mistakes with Jubal, but she loved her daughter more than her own life. Everything, every waking minute of her days and nights had been directed to caring for Melanie, to seeing that she had love and shelter.

"Don't insult me with that sort of question, Jubal. Of course I wanted her to have a father! And I can't begin to count the times I've wished I'd gotten involved with any man besides you. But I wasn't about to throw my daughter into some sort of three-parent and half-sibling situation with you and Evette that would be even more confusing to her. That is, assuming your wife would have accepted a child of yours from another woman," she added bitterly.

His lips flattened to a grim line. "So you think it was right for you to make all these decisions on your own? Well, let me give you this news flash, that's going to change. Starting now!"

Before she could ask him what that meant, he turned on his boot heel and marched out of the kitchen. Angela raced after him.

"Where are you going?" she demanded, as he picked up his hat and jacket. If he had any ideas about going over to the Sanchezes and telling Melanie that he was her father, she didn't know what she would do.

"Home," he said bluntly. He slapped on the hat and levered the brim down on his forehead. "I'm hardly in the mood for supper now."

Relieved and disappointed at the same time, Angela swallowed at the lump in her throat. "I suppose I should have waited until after we ate to tell you everything."

He let out a mocking laugh. "No. Waiting wouldn't have made anything better. You've already done way too much of that."

For a second Angela considered picking up the poinsettia and throwing it straight at his head. Did he realize how hard this was for her? Did he realize what a leap of faith she'd taken by making the decision to finally tell him the truth? But she just as quickly tempered the urge. Jubal was right. She had waited far too long to bring the truth out in the open. But she'd been afraid that any chance for a future with the man would be torn to shreds. And from the look of things, she'd been right.

"Saying I'm sorry again won't make things better," she said quietly. "I only ask that you try to understand my situation back then. Just like you wanted me to understand yours."

His hand on the doorknob, he paused long enough to dart her a dismal glance. "This—it's changed everything, Angie. I honestly don't know now how I feel about you—us."

Pain cut through the middle of her chest while tears burned her throat and eyes. In the past, she'd often imagined how things might have been if Jubal had been her husband when she'd given birth to Melanie. She'd always pictured him by her side, happy and proud, expressing his love for his wife and daughter. What a rose-colored dream that had been, she thought sadly.

"Melanie or not, I'm still the same woman that you made love to a few days ago, Jubal. Or am I no more than Evette was to you—just a partner for casual sex?"

If misery could have been put into human form, she was seeing it on Jubal's face as he jerked open the door. "That doesn't warrant an answer," he muttered, then quickly stepped over the threshold and shut the door behind him.

Feeling as though her feet had been knocked from beneath her, she walked shakily back into the kitchen and stared at the table set for two, the candles she'd intended to light. She'd been a complete and utter fool to think that Jubal might want to celebrate the fact that he was Melanie's father.

Ten days later, the Saddler house was brimming with guests for the first Sandbur holiday party. Angela, wearing an apron over her shirt and jeans, was racing about the kitchen, helping Cook arrange trays of hors d' oeuvres.

She'd been working since five this morning and now it was close to nine in the evening. She didn't have time to think about being exhausted. Nor did she have time to think about Jubal, who was out there in the living room, nibbling on delicacies and drinking expensive spirits with the rest of the party guests.

Even if she did have time to think of the man, her heart was too numb to hurt anymore. Since he'd left her house, she'd neither seen nor heard from the man. Maybe that was to be expected. After all, in his eyes, she'd done him wrong. But it was Melanie she was thinking about. Jubal knew he was her father now. She'd thought, hoped, that he would want to step up to that responsibility, that he would surely want to spend time with the child. Apparently, she'd misjudged the man.

The swinging door to the kitchen squeaked on its hinges and Angela looked up just in time to see Lex sauntering through the door. The blond-headed rancher looked exceptionally dashing tonight in a dark, western-cut suit and turquoise and silver bola tie. Angela had often wondered just what sort of woman it would take to capture his heart, but if the flirtatious grin on his face was any sign, he didn't have plans to settle down anytime soon.

"Well, well, this is where I should have been all along," he said. "The best looking women at the party are back here."

"We're not *at* the party, Lex," Cook pointed out dryly. "We're back here *making* the party. At least, the part you're eating. And I'll bet you've been doing plenty of that."

He sauntered over to Cook and reached over her shoulder to poke his finger into a bowl of shrimp dip. She promptly rapped his hand with a metal spatula.

"Get out of here!" she scolded. "That hand has been in cow manure!"

"Cook, honey, it's Saturday," he told her. "I took a shower before I got dressed."

"Let me see those fingernails," she ordered as she grabbed up Lex's hand for closer examination. "I'll bet they got dirt under 'em."

Lex looked over at Angela and winked. "When I was little Cook used to chase me back upstairs to wash. I didn't much like being clean then. Boys must be boys. But she can't get it through her head that I'm all grown up now."

"You'll never grow up," Cook spat back at him. Satisfied his nails were clean, she dropped his hand and went back to the dip she was mixing. "Why aren't you out there dancing with some of those high society women?"

Lex laughed. "Cause there's not one out there that can carry on a conversation without the word 'I' in every sentence."

"Since when were you interested in talking?" Cook retorted.

Laughing again, he stuck his head over Cook's shoulder and smacked a kiss on her cheek. "I only wish you were twenty years younger, Hattie. We'd cut a rug together."

Cook snorted, but Angela could see a look of fondness soften her features.

"That would only make me about fifty-two," she pointed out.

"Just perfect," he told her. "I like older women."

Hefting the spatula at him again, she ordered, "Get back to the front of the house, where you belong."

Turning away from Cook, he ambled over to Angela. "Actually, it's you, my dear, that drew me back here to the kitchen. Take off that apron and let's go have a dance."

Angela's mouth fell open. "Dance! Lex, I can't. Cook needs help and I look—" She glanced down at her jeans. One thigh was spotted with cooking oil, the other with a streak of red food coloring. Her hair was pulled into a messy ponytail and her face hadn't seen makeup in days. "Well, your mother would just die if I showed up in front of her guests like this."

"Mother won't care and if she does, I'll give her what for."

Grabbing her hand, he tugged her toward the door. Angela cast Cook a pleading glance. "Tell him I can't go, Cook!"

Cook chuckled. "I can't tell the boy anything."

Once Lex had her through the door, he led her down the long hallway that would take them to the living room. Even from this distance, she could hear bursts of laughter over the sound of music. Jubal would be in there, she thought desperately. She didn't want to see him! Not like this! In front of a group of people!

They were almost to the entrance to the living room when her feet stopped and Lex turned impatiently back to her.

"What's wrong?" he asked.

"I don't want to go in there, Lex. I look awful. And I—I wasn't invited."

"Yes, you are. I'm inviting you. Damn it, woman, I've

never had this much trouble getting a woman to dance with me. Don't bust my ego now. Cook will never let me live it down."

He was teasing her, playfully trying to put her at ease and Angela couldn't keep arguing with the man. After all, he was one of the many who signed her paycheck.

"All right. But just one dance and then I'm back to the kitchen," she reluctantly agreed.

Unfortunately, when they entered the living room, the live-band ended the song they'd been playing. Lex and Angie stood on the outskirts of the crowd as they waited for the next song to begin.

Realizing she was still wearing her apron, Angela began to fiddle with the tie at the back. "I forgot my apron," she told Lex. "I can't dance with this thing on."

"Here. Let me help," he gallantly offered.

He turned her around and quickly untied the two white strings that were wrapped around her waist and knotted at the back. Once he'd loosened it, she pulled off the dirty garment, then looked around for a place to stash it.

"I see the perfect place for that thing," Lex said, then grabbing the apron from her, he walked over and stuffed it inside a piano stool.

Angela was trying not to laugh when she spotted Jubal standing across the room, dressed regally in a dark suit and black boots. Like a laser honing in on a spot to cut, his gaze zeroed in on her and even from the distance of several feet, she could see he didn't look any happier than he had days ago when she'd told him he was a father.

Her heart aching, she told herself to look away, to put her mind on anything but him. She was actually glad when Lex returned to her side and the music started to play.

"Well, this must be my lucky night," he said, as the slow melody drifted across the room. "I can actually hold you in my arms."

"Lex, you are a hopeless flirt. And I don't know why you bothered dragging me out here when the room is full of pretty ladies."

He smiled down at her as they began to move to the music. "Maybe I thought you needed a little Christmas entertaining." His expression turned unusually serious. "You're always working, Angie. Don't you ever want to play and have fun?"

She glanced away from him and noticed that several of the guests were watching them. No doubt they all wondered what the prince of the ranch was doing dancing with the hired help. "Of course. But I don't always have the chance."

"Then we need to give you more chances. You're too young to always be holed away in the kitchen." His eyes narrowed with speculation. "Some of the wranglers tell me you've been on a few dates with Jubal. Cook mentioned it, too."

Her lips pressed together. "Since when has Cook started gossiping?"

"Don't blame Cook. I pried it out of her." He looked down at her. "Jubal's a good man. Moody, though. This past week he's been hell to work around. Guess he's one of those poor folks that would like to forget the holiday. I'm surprised he showed up tonight. I guess he did out of respect for Mother. She has a knack for bringing out the best in the worst."

Angela barely heard him—she was remembering when she and Melanie had helped him trim the tree. He'd seemed to take such delight in making it beautiful, and had been so thoughtful to let Melanie place the angel on top. The child was still talking about that day, about Jubal and about the Christmas tree. Each time her daughter brought up the subject, Angela's heart broke just that much more.

"I wouldn't say Jubal was the worst," she commented.

"Oh. Stickin' up for the guy, are you?"

She was about to tell him that she wanted to drop the subject of Jubal Jamison completely, when suddenly the man himself appeared directly behind Lex and tapped him on the shoulder.

"Sorry, I'm taking over," he told the other man.

Grinning affably, Lex stepped back from Angela and bowed toward Jubal. "By all means."

Angela's heart was throbbing so loudly in her ears that she hardly noticed Lex moving away and disappearing into the crowd, or that the music was still playing.

Standing with her arms rigidly against her sides, she stared blankly at Jubal as she waited for him to explain why he'd cut in on the dance. But no words came out of his mouth as he took her by the hand and drew her into his arms.

Her body stiff, she automatically began to follow his steps. But her mind was whirling, wondering what he could be up to. One thing was certain, he still had the power to hurt her.

"What are you doing out here?" he finally asked.

Burned by the insulting question, her head reared back to look at him. Years ago, she'd never thought of him as a snob, but after he'd chosen to marry Evette, a tiny part of her had wondered if it was because Angela had been a poor country girl without the social graces his family had been accustomed to.

"What's wrong?" she asked. "Does it embarrass you for

the cinder girl to come out of the kitchen and dare to show her face on the dance floor?"

His jaw tightened. "That's not what I meant. What were you doing dancing with Lex?"

Her brows shot innocently upward. "Is that a crime? Lex invited me. And I happen to like him."

A muscle jumped in his cheek. "Yes. I could see that."

Damn, damn, she silently cursed. Why did he have to look so good, feel so good? Why did she have to love him so?

"Don't act jealous, Jubal. It doesn't fit you."

"Is that why you think I cut in on the dance? Because I'm jealous?" he asked dryly.

"No. The key word is *act,* Jubal. A person has to actually care about someone before they can truly be jealous. You don't fit that bill, either."

She didn't know why she was being so waspish with him. It certainly wasn't the way to endear herself to the man. But for a week and a half now he'd ignored her and Melanie as though they meant nothing to him.

"You think you have the answers to everything, don't you?" he asked quietly.

Her hand was beginning to sweat against his, but he was holding her fingers so tightly that she couldn't have pulled them away even if she'd wanted to. He'd said he didn't know how he felt about her anymore, so what was he trying tell her now?

"If I had all the answers," she told him. "I would have never given you the time of day five years ago. I could have foreseen the heartache you were going to put me through and run like a scalded cat."

He didn't reply. Angela silently prayed for the song to end, for this torture of being in his arms to end.

"I cut in on the dance because I wanted to talk with you."

"There are telephones, Jubal," she said with undisguised sarcasm. "Or has yours been on the blink?"

Frowning, he muttered, "I think we should head outside for a little fresh air."

Unwilling to yank away from him and make a scene, she allowed him to lead her away from the other dancers and out the front door.

Thankfully the evening was mild and the massive house blocked out a faint, northerly breeze. At the moment there were only three other people standing on the porch, one man smoking a cigarette and another couple admiring the Christmas lights wrapped around every tree trunk in the yard.

Jubal drew her to the far end of the porch, away from the others. When he finally came to a stop at the edge of the low concrete and turned to her, she said, "You can let go of me now. I'm not going to run away."

Grimacing, he dropped his grip on her arm. "I tried calling you the last two evenings. You didn't answer."

"I wasn't home. I've had to work late the last two nights." The doubt on his face prompted her to add, "I don't have caller ID if that's what you're thinking. I wouldn't be so childish as to not pick up your calls."

He let out a long breath. "I wasn't sure. I called Geraldine—just to double-check that you or Melanie hadn't taken ill."

At least he'd shown a basic regard for their welfare, although it was hardly the same as coming to check on them in person. Yet, Angela wasn't going to brood on that miserable thought now. The last thing she wanted to do was break down in tears in front of the man. Especially when she had to go back to the kitchen soon and face Cook. The woman already wanted to kick Jubal right off the Sandbur and yell good riddance after him.

"So. You wanted to say something to me?" she asked.

Jubal couldn't understand any of it. The Saddler house was full of beautiful women, most of them dressed in diamonds and fancy cocktail dresses that cost more than Angela probably made in a whole month. They were all what his parents would call "nice, suitable women" but not one of them could spark his interest. Not one of them made his gut churn with longing, his knees weak, his breath catch. Only Angela could do that. It didn't matter that she was dressed in work clothes, that her hair was a mess, her lips bare. She looked sexy and gorgeous and the moment he'd spotted her with Lex, jealously had stabbed him like a barbed lance.

He swallowed. "Yes. I'd like to see Melanie. To take her out to my house for a few hours tomorrow. Is that agreeable with you?"

He was relieved when she didn't waver.

"Of course. I'm sure she'll be excited to see you again."

For some reason his throat felt raw and the urge to grab her and pull her into his arms kept flashing through his mind.

That's stupid, Jubal. The woman deceived you. She kept your child from you for nearly five years. She's no better than Evette. You can't still love her, want her!

Blocking out the pestering voice in his head, he said, "Well, my cat had kittens and I thought Melanie would like to see them."

She lifted her arms to tighten her ponytail. Jubal's gaze automatically dropped to the thrust of her breasts. Had it been only days ago that he'd touched her naked skin, kissed every inch of her? It felt like forever.

"I didn't know you had a cat," she said.

He shrugged. "If you have a barn, you have to have a cat. And I guess Miss Kitty thought she had to have babies."

"Mel would love to see the kittens."

She moistened her lips and he forced himself to look away. For the past ten days he'd been torn between wanting her and keeping his distance, trying to come to terms with what she'd done and his own guilt for not being there for her when she'd needed him the most.

"I expect you to come with her," he said after a moment.

When she didn't immediately reply, he glanced back to see she was staring skeptically at him.

"I—I'm not sure that's a good idea, Jubal. I'm not sure we're ready for each other's company. I'll stay home and you can entertain Mel for as long as you like."

Her words were polite, but cool and Jubal felt as though she'd just erected a wall of ice between them. Even though he was angry and hurt, he still hated the separation. Hated the coldness. "No. Melanie doesn't know me well enough for that."

She sighed. "Maybe you're right."

"Then you'll come, too?"

She shrugged. "I want Melanie to know her father. So I'll do what I have to do."

That wasn't exactly the response he'd hoped to hear. But then he wasn't exactly sure what he needed or wanted to hear Angela say. Since her revelation about Melanie, he'd gone around like a zombie, wondering what had happened to the plans he'd made for the future. He'd wanted Angela and Melanie to be a part of his life, for the three of them to be a family. Learning that Melanie was actually his true daughter should have made those plans even more perfect.

Instead, it had cracked the foundation he'd been standing on. If Angela was capable of keeping something that important from him, what else might she hide from him? Dear God, he didn't know what to think anymore.

"All right. I'll pick you up tomorrow at two," he said.

She shook her head. "There's no need for that. I'll drive the two of us over to your place. Now, if you'll excuse me, I have to get back to work. Cook needs me in the kitchen."

She swished past him, leaving her scent trailing after her. He watched her walk past the front door of the house, on past the star-gazing couple, then off the porch to disappear into the darkness.

Apparently she was walking around the outside of the house to avoid going back through the party. The fact struck him right in the middle of the chest. She'd never felt as though she belonged to his social circle. And obviously she didn't even feel as though she belonged at a Sandbur party. As long as he'd known her, she'd been a loner, fiercely independent and proud. Was that part of the reason she'd not come to him when she'd discovered she was pregnant? Because she felt she didn't fit in his world? No matter, she should have. And that was the thing he couldn't forget.

Chapter Twelve

By the time Sunday afternoon rolled around, the skies had turned overcast, but the weather was warm enough to forget about coats.

As Angela buttoned a thin sweater over Melanie's T-shirt, the child squirmed and giggled and chattered nonstop about the upcoming visit with Jubal.

"I want to take my books, Mommy. Jubal will read to me. He likes the story about the elephant. He told me so."

"Really? That's nice."

"And he likes the one about the pony, too. 'Cause Jubal takes care of animals. He makes them better when they're sick."

Pausing in her task, Angela studied her daughter's cherub face. "You remember that about him?"

"Uh-huh. I remember everything."

Angela finished the last button and smoothed the hem

of the garment over Melanie's hips. "Is that so? What about brushing your teeth? Did you remember that, too?"

Nodding, Melanie curled back her lips and clamped her teeth together to allow her mother a closeup inspection. "See? They're clean."

"Beautiful," Angela agreed. "I think I should give you the smiley button for doing such a good job."

"Can I have a shiny horse, like you have?" Melanie asked.

Angela glanced down at the broach fixed to the left shoulder of her jersey top. She wasn't sure why she was wearing the gift from Jubal today. It was a bit masochistic, she supposed, since the man no longer appeared to love her. If he ever had, she added sadly. Maybe he'd never really meant any of the caring things he'd said to her. She didn't know what to think anymore.

"I don't have another shiny horse." And she didn't have a brown and white pony to put under the Christmas tree, either, she thought dismally. "You'll just have to settle for a smiley face."

For a moment Melanie seemed to consider whining, but then thought better of it. Angela went over to the desk and fished out the yellow smiley button pin that she used to reward her daughter for good behavior.

She had just finished pinning it to Melanie's sweater, when there was a light knock on the door.

Wondering if Jubal had changed his mind and come to fetch them after all, Angela hurried to door and was completely surprised to see Juliet standing on the porch.

The other woman smiled broadly. "Got a minute?"

"Juliet! Please, come in."

"I can't stay long. Matt's watching Jess and he lets him

get into anything and everything. They'll have the house torn apart if I don't get back soon," she said with a laugh.

How wonderful that must be, Angela thought. To have a husband, a family, a home where love dwelt. She wondered if Juliet realized how very blessed she was to have Matt and two beautiful children.

Angela gestured toward the couch. "Would you like something to drink? There's coffee still in the pot."

"No thanks. We just finished lunch a few minutes ago."

When Juliet sank onto the couch and crossed her legs, Melanie made a beeline to the other woman. Juliet hugged the child close, then patted the top of her head.

"Where's Jess? Didn't he wanta come see me?" Melanie asked.

Juliet laughed. "He doesn't know I'm here. His daddy is keeping him occupied."

"Oh. What's occ—occapied?"

Laughing again, Juliet said, "That means busy and out of trouble. Wow, but you look all pretty today. Did your mother braid your hair?"

Melanie reached up and tugged the two pigtails hanging over each ear. "Yep. She did."

"And she tied ribbons at the ends. That's just the way I always liked mine."

Melanie did a little preening twirl in front of their guest. "I'm gonna go see Jubal today. He has a big Christmas tree with lights and an angel."

"How nice." Juliet glanced shrewdly at Angela. "That sounds hopeful."

Angela quickly took Melanie by the shoulder and headed her in the direction of the bedroom. "Go gather your books together, honey. We'll be leaving in a few minutes."

The child raced out of the room and Angela spoke in a voice low enough that Melanie couldn't hear. "He only wants to see Melanie."

Juliet surveyed Angela's face, which had grown thin and angled in the past couple of weeks.

"I take it you've told him that he's Melanie's father."

Angela sighed. "He resents me, Juliet. But then I shouldn't expect anything else from him, I suppose."

Disgusted, Juliet said under her breath, "Why the hell not? You're the mother of his child. If for no other reason than that, he should be treating you with respect."

Rising to her feet, Angela moved aimlessly around the small living room. A few months ago, she'd moved onto the Sandbur and into this house, believing and hoping that this was a new beginning for her. Now it seemed more like the end of everything.

"I suppose I've shattered his trust in me," Angela said wearily. "I tried to explain my reasons, but he couldn't understand them anymore than I could understand his marrying Evette."

Juliet shook her head. "The man is in no position to judge anyone—particularly you." Rising, Juliet walked over to Angela and put a consoling hand on her shoulder. "Both Cook and I are worried about you. We know we're sticking our noses into something that is none of our business, but we love you, honey, and we hate seeing you like this. Frankly, you look like you've gone to hell and back."

"Thanks," Angela said wryly. "That makes me feel much better about things."

Juliet rolled her eyes. "Seriously, what are you going to do about this?"

Angela's heart was so heavy, she wondered how it kept

beating. "I can't make him love me, Juliet. And I can't make him forgive me. I can only hope that as time passes, he'll become a good father to Melanie."

Juliet looked as though she wanted to give Angela a dose of sage advice, but then her expression changed to one of curiosity as her gaze caught on the broach pinned to Angela's sweater. Leaning closer, she inspected the glittery figure.

"Pins are my very favorite pieces of jewelry and this piece is gorgeous. Where did you get it?"

Angela sighed. "Jubal gave it to me a while back, before—well, before he found out about Melanie. It's just a trinket, but I like it."

Juliet laughed. "Trinket! Angie, honey, you'd better go get under a light and take a closer look. These are real gems. Diamonds, emeralds, rubies. I imagine that little 'trinket' as you call it, set his wallet back quite a bit. But he can afford it. God knows the ranch is paying him a fortune."

Stunned, Angela looked down at the little horse. "Real? It can't be." It wasn't any more real than his love had ever been, she thought ruefully.

"Don't take my word for it," Juliet told her. "Take it to a jeweler's and find out for yourself."

"Is that what you would do?" Angela asked with a frown.

Juliet chuckled. "No. I'm happy if Matt gives me a toy out of the Cracker Jack box. I treasure all of his gifts."

And so would Angela, as long as they were given with love. But she seriously doubted that Jubal would ever be giving her anything again, especially his love.

She was staring thoughtfully into space when Juliet leaned forward and kissed her cheek. "I'd better go, honey. Call me later. I want to talk to you about spending Christmas with us. It would be great for Melanie to be with the kids."

Angela nodded. "All right. I'll call. And thanks, Juliet, for caring enough to stop by."

Fifteen minutes later, after borrowing Geraldine's work truck to drive over the rough road to Jubal's, she parked beneath the shade tree and reached to unfasten Melanie from her booster seat.

"Need help?"

Glancing over her shoulder, she saw that Jubal was already standing outside of the vehicle. Even with the brim of his hat shading most his face, she could see his expression was distant.

Stifling a sigh, she said, "No thanks. I can do it."

Once she and Melanie were safely on the ground, Melanie ran straight to Jubal and flung her arms around his legs.

Bittersweet pangs struck Angela's heart. It was uncanny how the girl had taken to Jubal, almost like she knew he was an important person in her life.

"Hi there, beautiful!" Jubal greeted as he bent down and swooped Melanie up in his arms.

Like a dog sensing it was loved, the child wrapped her arms trustingly around his neck. "I brought books and my dolly. I want to show her the Christmas tree."

Jubal's smile for his daughter was warm and tender—a sight that relieved Angela greatly. No matter what had happened in the past, Melanie deserved his love.

"Then we'd better go right in," he said to Melanie.

Trying not to feel left out, Angela gathered up her tote bag from the floorboard of the truck and followed the two of them into the house.

Because of the warm weather, there was no fire in the fire place, but the lights on the Christmas tree were burning and the smell of cinnamon emanated from the kitchen. Although only one person lived in it, the house felt homey.

Did he ever feel lonely, Angela wondered, as lonely as she felt with no head resting on the pillow next to hers at night? Dear God, don't me her think about those things now, she prayed. If she did, she might just break into sobs right in front of the man.

The minute Jubal set Melanie on her feet, the child went straight to the tree and tilted her head back as far as it would possibly go. Jubal followed.

"The angel is still there," she proudly announced. "She's watchin' over us."

"Who told you that?" Jubal asked.

"Cook. She says angels are always watchin' over us. So we'll be safe."

"I think Cook is probably right," he murmured, then glanced over at Angela, who was still standing awkwardly in the middle of the living room. "Uh—make yourself comfortable, Angie."

Trying not to appear as stiff as she felt, she walked over to an armchair and sank onto the seat. Melanie immediately ran over to her. "Can I have Beatrice, Mommy? So I can show her the bootiful tree."

Angela gave her the doll and while the child carried the toy across the room and away from the adults, Jubal moved over to Angela's chair.

"Beatrice?" he asked curiously. "Where did that come from?"

"It's from a cartoon program she watches in the evenings."

With one hand, he gestured about the room. "You can see that I'm not a TV person. Guess I'll have to get one for little muffin's sake."

"That isn't necessary," Angela said. "I don't allow her to watch that much television anyway. I like for her to use her own imagination rather than have someone else do it for her."

His gaze pinned her to the armchair. "Have you stopped to think that I might want to have some say in what Melanie does or doesn't do in the future?"

He didn't exactly sound angry, but there was a sharpness to his tone that cut her anyway. She did her best not to let him see that deep down she was falling apart, aching for things between them to be right and good.

She swallowed. "Yes, I have thought about it. Do you…plan to see her often?"

The question appeared to insult him, but she couldn't help that. If she didn't ask him things directly, then how would she know exactly where they stood with this parenting problem? These past few days, he'd not exactly let her in on his thoughts or his plans. He ought to know she needed answers.

"You mean, just how much of a dad do I plan to be?"

Angela gave him a brief nod. "I guess that's what I'm trying to ask."

His face remained an unreadable mask. "I plan to be as much of a father to Melanie as possible—without you and me living together under the same roof."

He might as well have picked up a knife and stabbed her with it, Angela thought. The pain in her chest made it difficult to breathe, but she somehow managed to give him a faint smile. "That shouldn't be a problem. We don't live far apart. I only wish—" She broke off suddenly as she realized she'd been on the verge of telling him she wished things could be different between them. But she wasn't going to intimate anything that revealing to the man. He'd obviously thought about his feelings toward her and had decided they weren't strong enough for anything like marriage.

His eyes narrowed skeptically. "What?"

"Nothing," she answered quickly. "I just wanted to say that I know you'll be a good father to her. And I'm—glad that the two of you are together. Truly."

For a few, brief seconds, his features softened. "Thank you for that much," he said, then turned and walked across the room to where their daughter was playing with her doll beneath the Christmas tree.

After that, Jubal focused all of his attention on their child, leaving Angela to entertain herself. Eventually, while Jubal read storybooks to Melanie, she wandered back to the kitchen and made a pot of coffee. She was sitting at a small oak table, sipping the brew, when Jubal entered the room.

She looked up at the sound of his footsteps, expecting to see Melanie following right behind him. Instead, he was alone and from the odd look on his face, she figured he must be annoyed that he'd been forced to include her in this gathering today. The idea crushed her.

"I hope you don't mind," she said. "I took the liberty of looking in the cabinets for the coffee and a filter."

Jamming his hands in the pockets of his jeans, he walked over to her. "Of course, I don't mind."

How could they have gone from sharing a bed together to this stiff awkwardness? she wondered. It was stupid. But she didn't know how to change things back. Maybe it was too late. Maybe she was meant to live the rest of her life with a broken heart. It wouldn't be that difficult. She already had five years of practice.

Releasing a long breath, she gestured toward the coffee maker on the cabinet counter. "Would you like a cup?"

He hesitated for a moment, then shook his head. "Melanie is waiting on the porch for me to take her to the barn. I came to see if you'd like to come with us."

Angela realized it didn't matter why he was inviting her to join the two of them, only that he had. "Sure. Let me put my cup away."

He waited for Angela at the open doorway, then gestured for her to proceed out of the house. As she walked ahead of him, she was acutely aware of his presence and how different, how terribly sad she felt compared to the last time she'd been in this house.

He'd made love to her then. Slow, sweet and heart-wrenching love. He'd touched her with passion. Now he didn't seem to want to touch her at all. How could a person stop feeling, wanting, she wondered. She certainly didn't know how.

The barn was located to the west of the house, about a hundred feet away. It was made of lumber and roofed with corrugated iron. A porch was attached to the front and covered a small pen that presently housed one palomino horse.

As the three of them moved into the dimly lit barn, Angela was surprised to see that a portion of the interior was floored with wide pine planks, worn smooth by years of footsteps. In this area, bales of alfalfa hay were stacked neatly all the way to the ceiling. On the opposite side of the structure were several wire pens, one of which held two small gray Brahman calves.

"Miss Kitty is over here, behind a bale of hay," Jubal told Melanie as he took her hand and led her forward. "But you must be quiet and still when you look at the kittens.

Otherwise, Miss Kitty will get frightened and carry them away. Can you do that?"

Clearly insulted by his insinuation, Melanie frowned up at him. "I know how to be quiet. But Jess don't. He hollers and cries. 'Cause he's a baby. But I'm not a baby anymore."

Jubal glanced over his shoulder at Angela who was following a couple of steps behind them. His expression was full of wry amusement and the sight warmed her. Perhaps they could do this parenting thing together after all, she thought hopefully. At least, it was a start.

"If Mel thinks she's grown up now, what will she be like as a teenager?" he wanted to know as Melanie ran ahead of them to explore.

His question broke enough of the ice between them to allow Angela to smile and she held her palms up in a helpless gesture. "I'm scared to think about those teenage years."

Yet Angela was even more scared to think about the future and the part he'd be playing in their lives. Right now, the best she could imagine was a mother and father, living in different homes, yet sharing equal custody of a child that had originally been conceived in love. It was far from the life she wanted for herself and her daughter, but at least it would be a start.

Pulling her thoughts back to the present, she realized that the three of them had come to the end of the haystack where several bales had been taken out to leave a short ledge.

Jubal lifted Melanie up onto the makeshift shelf and instructed her to sit down while he lifted Miss Kitty from her hidey-hole.

"Come here, girl," Jubal said softly to the cat as he sat

the animal in the open and gently stroked her back. "You've got company."

The gray and white long-haired cat blinked her eyes, then stared curiously at Melanie. Angela was wondering where the mother had stored her babies, when several tiny meows sounded from a crack in the hay. Seconds later, three miniature replicas of Miss Kitty poked their bobbing heads into the open.

As soon as Melanie spotted them, she let out an excited squeal that sent the furry little creatures running for cover. Seeing what she'd done, her mouth opened wide, and she plopped a hand over it.

"Oh. I forgot!"

"Sssh," Jubal urged. "They'll come back."

He was right. Only a minute or two passed before the babies' curiosity got the better of them and they ventured out of their hiding place again. Instinctively, Angela moved forward for a better look at the adorable kittens.

"They're beautiful balls of fur," Angela whispered to Jubal. "Where ever did you get the mother?"

"She just came here one day while I was moving my things into the house. Later, I asked some of the guys if they'd ever seen her around the ranch yard. None of them had, so I don't know. She must have traveled miles from somewhere to make her home here. I could see she was heavy with kittens and I couldn't turn her away."

A lump as big as Texas suddenly moved into Angela's throat. If he'd not found it in his heart to turn away a pregnant cat, then he most certainly would have moved mountains to care for her and his coming child if she'd had the courage to turn to him back then. In spite of Evette and her selfish manipulations, Angela had been wrong in not going to him. Very wrong. Now she wondered if he'd ever give her the chance to make up for her mistake.

"Can I pet them?" Melanie whispered.

Moving his head close to the child's, Jubal whispered back, "You can try. But don't be sad if they run off again."

Still struggling to keep her emotions in check, Angela decided to leave the two of them alone with the kittens while she explored the rest of the barn.

Moving over to a wall near the right of the door, she studied several antique farm implements and wagon wheels hanging from rusty nails. Since the pieces appeared to have been there for years, she figured some of the Sandbur family had stored them there.

Not long after Angela had come to work for the ranch, Cook had told her quite a bit of the place's history. The estate had originated more than a century ago and had been handed down through many generations. The deep family connection was something Angela envied. Especially since she'd lost ties with her parents.

After a long inspection of the antiques, Angela ambled over to the pair of calves. At the moment, the two little beauties were curled up together on a bed of hay and appeared to be asleep. But when she stopped at the fence, they both lifted their heads and stared at her.

"So, what are you two doing here so far away from the herd and your mother?" she quietly asked the calves.

"The twins lost their mother. She died after giving birth to them."

The fact that Jubal had walked up behind her at some point surprised her as much as his sad information.

"Oh, how terrible," she murmured. Tears stung her eyes as she gazed at the orphaned calves, though she felt foolish for getting emotional. She understood that Mother Nature was often cruel. But sometimes it felt as though the cruelty of things was all she ever witnessed.

She heard him release a quiet sigh.

"The cow was a first-time mother and the hands didn't find her until she was already in deep trouble. I tried my best to save her. But it wasn't meant to be."

Even though there was no outward crack in his voice, she could hear the regret in his words and, surprisingly, a hint of guilt. Which had to be entirely unwarranted. If there was one thing she was certain of, Jubal was a dedicated veterinarian. He went above and beyond normal efforts to make sure his patients survived and thrived.

Without thinking, she turned slightly toward him and placed a hand on his forearm. "You can't feel responsible, Jubal. I'm sure you did your best."

She saw him glance at her fingers wrapped around his sleeve and she could tell that his thoughts were more occupied with her touch than her words.

"My best wasn't good enough," he murmured.

Was he talking about his effort with the cow or his relationship with her, Angela wondered, but she dared not ask. With Melanie present, now wasn't the time to confront him about their personal situation.

"You're a doctor, Jubal. Not a miracle worker." Dropping her hand from his arm, she looked to the calves. "You're taking care of them now," she reminded him.

He stepped close to her side and Angela's insides began to tremble with the urge to wrap her arms around him, to confess that all she ever wanted was to love him.

"I give them a bottle several times a day. The milk is filled with nutrients and made to mimic their mother's."

"Will they survive?" she couldn't help but ask.

"Oh, yes. They'll be fine. I'm not sure I will be though by the time they're old enough to eat grass and feed," he said with a bit of wry amusement.

"I'm sure some of the ranch hands would take over the job of nursing them," she suggested.

He gave his head a brief shake. "It's important to me that I do it." He slanted her a glance. "You understand, don't you?"

Tilting her gaze up to him, she searched his green eyes and felt her heart wince at the suffering she found there. Never had she wanted to hurt him. Just as he'd insisted he'd never wanted to hurt her. She could see that so clearly now. But what did *he* see?

"Yes. I understand," she said softly, then glanced over her shoulder at Melanie. The child was still sitting on the haystack, mesmerized by the three kittens playing around her. "Jubal, I think—" She swallowed, then tried again, "I've been thinking that if you're going to be spending time with Melanie that I—should tell her that you're her father. Or we could tell her together. Either way you want to handle it is fine with me."

Clearly surprised, he turned to face her. "Do you think she's ready?" he asked. "That she'd understand what you're telling her?"

Angela nodded. "She's very bright for her age, Jubal. But then you've probably already figured that out for yourself."

A half grin lifted the corner of his mouth and for the first time since she'd uncovered her secret about Melanie to him, she could plainly see pride on his face. The sight filled her heart, pulled her to him in the most intimate kind of way. Melanie was the connection between them that could never be broken.

"Okay," he agreed. Glancing thoughtfully over to their daughter, he added, "I think you should be the one to explain it to her first. After all, you've been her sole parent for all this time. You're the one she looks to for guidance and security. Hearing it from you might make it easier for her to understand."

A breath of relief rushed past Angela's lips. "I hope so. I'll try my best to do it right. I want her to love you as much as—well, as much as any little girl can love her father."

Before Jubal could stop himself, his head bent and his lips captured hers. The familiar taste of her mouth swamped him with feelings that he'd been desperately trying to tamp down all afternoon. Before he finally managed to step back, he felt his whole body go hard with longing.

Drawing in a long breath, he said, "I don't know why I did that."

Liar. You did it because you wanted to. Because loving her is all you've ever wanted to do.

She pressed her lips together and glanced away from him, but Jubal could see the kiss had shaken her as much as it had him. Her breasts were rising and falling as though she'd been running and his racing heart felt as though he'd been running right along with her.

"I don't know why you did, either," she said quietly.

What was happening to him, Jubal wondered. For the past two weeks, he'd been living behind a wall of cold resentment and no matter how he'd tried to rationalize Angela's decision to keep Melanie's birth from him, his heart had remained closed and hurt.

Now as he looked at her sad face, he felt a part of that

wall beginning to crack and melt. Was he one big chump or was he just now learning what it was like to really forgive? Forgive her? And most of all, forgive himself?

Chapter Thirteen

"It's getting dark," he said as he glanced away from Angela to the front of the barn. "We'd better go in. Would you and Melanie like to eat something before you go?"

Angela stepped away from the wire fence as she tried to gather her wits back together. The kiss he'd planted on her lips only moments before had been completely unexpected and try as she might, she couldn't figure out what was going on inside his head. Was he trying to tell her that he still cared for her? No. She didn't want to think that, to allow herself to hope, only to have it dashed back in her face.

"That isn't necessary," she said politely. "I wouldn't want to put you out."

He actually smiled. "It's only sandwiches, Angie. Nothing special."

An hour later, after helping him clean away the simple meal, Angela and Melanie told him good-bye. As she drove the two of them away from the ranch house, she didn't look back, but she somehow knew he was standing on the porch, watching their departure.

The image stabbed her so deeply that for several minutes she considered turning around and going back to him. What harm would it do if she told him that she still loved him, that all she wanted was for the three of them to be together? All he could do was reject her and that had already happened twice before. Maybe a third time would be different.

No. Now wasn't the time to lay her heart on the line to him, she decided. The day had been long and it was going to be Melanie's bedtime soon.

She absently fingered the broach on her shoulder. There would be another chance, another day to try to reason with Jubal. Right now, she needed to figure out the best way to tell Melanie about her father.

Once they got home, Angela helped Melanie put away her books and doll, then had the girl change into her pajamas and brush her teeth.

After a few minutes Melanie came running out to the living room and bounded onto the cushion next to her mother.

"I'm all finished, Mommy! Can I stay up and watch television with you? Pretty please?"

"I'm not going to watch television. I'm going to take a bath."

Disappointment puckered her little features. "Then can I eat cookies and drink milk?"

Knowing a stalling tactic when she heard one, Angela said, "No. You just finished eating over at Jubal's. Besides, I want to talk to you about something."

Wide-eyed, Melanie bounced on the cushion. "Are you

gonna put up our Christmas tree now? I bet it won't look as pretty as Jubal's."

Angela had been so busy helping Cook prepare for parties that she'd barely had time to buy a few gifts and a small artificial tree. Tomorrow evening, she decided, she would make a point in erecting the tree and letting Melanie help her with the decorations.

"What makes you say that?" she asked the child.

She stuck her little nose high in the air. "Because Jubal's tree is the prettiest tree ever and there's angels all around it."

Angela darted a puzzled glance at her. "There's only one angel on Jubal's tree, honey. The one you placed on the top."

Melanie swished her head back and forth. "No. There was this many angels." She held up three fingers. "And they were dancing and singing."

Well, at least the child had a vivid imagination, Angela thought. She patted her lap. "Come here, honey."

The girl happily climbed onto her lap and Angela slowly began to undo her braids.

"Mel, do you remember when I talked to you about your daddy?"

She nodded. "Mmm-hmm. You said that he lived far away and couldn't see us."

Angela winced. Dear God, the decision she'd made so long ago hadn't just affected Jubal, it had also caused their daughter to miss out on so much.

Tenderly brushing the stray hairs away from Melanie's forehead, she said, "That's right. But now—well, things have changed. Your Daddy has moved close to us and we…we can see him now."

Confusion, bewilderment, then pure joy danced across

Melanie's face and then her mouth formed a tiny O. "We can see him? Like I went to see Santa Claus?"

Tears were suddenly burning Angela's throat. "Well," she began, carefully trying to choose her words carefully, "that's what I wanted to tell you. You saw your daddy today. Jubal is your daddy."

As soon as the announcement was out, she could see the wheels in Melanie's head working at full speed. Angela was wondering what the child could possibly be thinking and how she was absorbing the news, when Melanie suddenly leaped off her lap and began to jump up and down in the middle of the floor.

"Jubal is my daddy! Jubal is my daddy!" she shouted gleefully.

Angela let the girl continue her celebration dance for a few more seconds before she called her back to her side. As Melanie sidled up to Angela's knee, she was grinning from ear to ear. It seemed almost ridiculous to ask her how she felt about the news.

"Are you really happy about this, Mel?"

"Yeah! Yeah! Jubal is nice and big and strong."

Three important attributes for little princesses, Angela thought wryly. Hopefully when Melanie grew older she'd have a whole list of reasons why she loved having Jubal for a father. But for now just seeing her daughter's jubilant face filled her heart with more joy than she'd felt in years.

"Yes, he is," Angela agreed.

Melanie suddenly raced away from her mother's side and climbed up on a chair to grab something from the desk where Angela studied. When she climbed down and ran back to her mother, Angela could see car keys dangling from her little hand.

"Here, Mommy. Can we get in the car and go see him?" she asked as she handed the set of keys to her mother.

With a brief shake of her head, Angela tried to reason, "Honey, we just saw Jubal. It's getting too late to go back to his house tonight."

Tilting her head to one side, Melanie gave her mother a comical look. "But Mommy, I want to sleep in my daddy's house. Jess sleeps in his daddy's house. And so does Marti and Gracia. Now I can, too!"

Hearing a stubborn streak threaded in the last of her daughter's words, Angela feared she was in for an argument.

"Darling, listen to me. There will be times when you can sleep in your daddy's house. But tonight isn't one of them. Sometimes mommies and daddies live in separate houses. Like me and Jubal. So—that makes things different." And sad, Angela thought. So sad and wasteful.

Clearly upset, Melanie marched to the middle of the room and stomped both feet. "I wanta go! I wanta be with my daddy tonight!" Angela could see that Melanie had started to cry.

Leaving the couch, Angela picked up the tearful child and carried her to her bedroom. After tucking her beneath the covers, she eased down on the edge of the bed, and kissed Melanie's blotchy cheek.

If only she could wave a wand and make everything instantly right for her daughter, she thought, as she smoothed a hand over the child's forehead. But it was going to take more than magic to fix all the things that had gone wrong between her and Jubal.

"There's no reason for you to be so upset, sweetheart. I'll take you to see Jubal tomorrow. But not if you keep acting naughty like you're doing now. Jubal would be very disappointed in you if he could see the way you're behaving."

Melanie's lips pressed mutinously together and she squeezed her eyes shut as a way of telling her mother she had no intention of carrying on a conversation with her now.

Angela didn't press her daughter to talk. Melanie needed time to digest the news she'd been given. She also needed to think about the unruly way she'd just behaved. Angela kissed her cheek one more time, then switched on the night light and left the bedroom.

After she locked the house for the night, she gathered a robe and headed to the bathroom. Initially, she'd planned to have a nice long bath, then enjoy a steaming cup of tea. But the ordeal with Melanie had left her drained and now all she wanted to do was have a quick wash under the shower, then lie down in front of the television and try to switch off all her troubled thoughts.

Fifteen minutes later, after combing the tangles from her wet hair, she came out of the bathroom and was searching for the television remote when she noticed a wooden footstool sitting near the door jamb.

Perplexed by the sight, she walked over to move it out of the way. The stool hardly ever left its position in a far corner of the room. In fact, the only time Angela ever used the piece of furniture was to reach high places. Had she used it earlier in the day and forgotten to put it away?

Angela reached the door and froze with horrified shock. The lock that bolted across the door was open.

Melanie! Oh God, no!

The silent prayer galvanized her into action and she raced down the hallway to Melanie's bedroom. The night light was still burning, but the bed was empty.

"Melanie! Where are you?"

The silence was even more shocking than the empty bed and, in the back of her mind, Angela realized her daughter was nowhere in the house. While she'd been in the shower, Melanie had crawled out of bed, unlocked the door and crept out in the night. Angela instantly knew that in her little mind, Melanie had decided that she was going to get to her daddy's house one way or the other.

Racing back out to the living room, Angela snatched up the telephone and dialed Jubal's number.

Two miles away, Jubal had just finished feeding the calves their bottles and was entering the house when his cell phone rang.

Stepping inside and shutting the door behind him, he pulled the instrument from his pocket and answered without bothering to look at the caller ID.

"Jubal."

He could hear a burst of breath on the other end and then Angela practically shouting his name. "Jubal! Oh thank God you answered. Melanie is gone! She's run away!"

Stunned, he stared blindly at the Christmas tree where his daughter had been playing only a couple of hours ago.

"What do you mean, *run away?*"

"Twenty minutes ago, while I was in the shower! She managed to unbolt the door and leave the house. She's—I'm sure she's trying to get to your place."

Closing his eyes, Jubal sent up a silent prayer. "Call Matt! I'll be right there!"

Jubal had been through a few frightening situations in his life, but nothing could be compared to the fear that was now chilling his very blood. If something happened to his daughter, his world would go black. Completely black.

Running on pure adrenaline, he was hardly aware of jumping into the truck and speeding toward Angie's house. As he steadily stomped on the gas, dust boiled behind him while startled rabbits and raccoons darted from his headlights.

It wasn't until the last half mile that he forced himself to slow down and begin to scan the road for any sign of Melanie. Trying to think clearly, he rationalized that a child of her size wouldn't be able to cover too much ground in twenty minutes. That meant the area between the horse barn and Angela's house would be the most likely place to find her. Unless the darkness had confused her and she'd headed south. Which would put her in wide open spaces with endless pastures full of bulls, rattlesnakes and God only knew what else.

When he reached Angela's house, he found her outside, searching her car with a flashlight. The moment he reached her, he grabbed her and held her tightly against his chest. Their past problems suddenly seemed trivial.

"I'm so sorry, Jubal," she sobbed. "I had told her about you—that you were her father. She was so happy that she wanted to go straight back to your house. I told her she'd have to wait until tomorrow and she got upset with me. I never dreamed she would sneak out of the house while I wasn't looking!"

As she explained what had happened, Jubal found himself stroking her hair, trying to absorb the frightened tremors racking her body. He didn't want this woman to ever hurt again. Not for any reason. "It's all right, Angie. Right now we've got to find her." He eased her out of his arms and looked down at her terror-stricken face. "Where have you looked for her?"

She was giving him the detailed answer to that question

when a pickup skidded to a halt next to Jubal's. Both of them turned to see Matt leap from the vehicle and quickly stride over to them.

"The boys down at the bunkhouse are gathering for a search party," he explained. "I drove over here thinking I might see Melanie on the way. How long has she been missing?"

Angela glanced at her watch. "Maybe thirty minutes at the most."

"I'm going back to search around our place. She might have headed there thinking she could see Jess." Matt jerked a cell phone from his jacket and quickly punched in a number. As soon as the person on the other end answered, the rancher began to bark out orders as he jogged back to his truck.

Jubal looked at Angela. "Let's comb the backyard, then head toward the ranch yard. I can't imagine her taking off to the south." His gaze swung toward the open wilderness. "There are no lights in that direction. Has she ever talked about wanting to see what was over there?"

Angela shook her heard. "No. And tonight, all she was talking about was seeing you. Spending the night with her daddy."

His face was suddenly pinched with cold and fright and most of all, regret. "I should have never let you leave tonight—either of you," he said hoarsely. "I should have kept you both with me."

Figuring it was fear doing his talking, Angela didn't question what he meant. There was no time for questions or regrets. They had to find their daughter.

Jubal grabbed a flashlight from his truck and the two of them hurried around to the back of the house to search behind every shrub and tree and shadowy corner.

After a handful of minutes passed without any luck, Angela said bleakly, "She's not here, Jubal. Even if she was hiding from me, she would have come out as soon as she heard your voice."

Nodding, he grabbed her by the arm and urged her to the front of the house. "Come on. Let's look at the edge of the road. If we're lucky, we might pick up her footprints. What sort of shoes would she be wearing, something that will leave a print?"

"I—I don't know. I left her in bed. She must be wearing her pajamas. But as for her shoes, the only ones she can manage on her own are her ballet slippers or cowboy boots. And the boots have slick soles."

He groaned. "Well, we'll look anyway. We might spot the heel marks."

Incredibly, they did find a few of Melanie's heel prints in the thick dust at the edge of the dirt road directly in front of the house. They followed them for about thirty feet before the road turned hard with crushed oyster shell which had been put there to help the ruts stand up to heavy traffic.

Angela let out a frustrated groan. "Now we don't know if she kept going straight down the road or turned off and waded into the weeds."

"Look around, Angela," he calmly instructed. "She would have had to follow the glow of the yard lights. Otherwise, it's too dark for her to find her way anywhere."

Feeling more confident, he grabbed her by the arm and urged her forward. He'd only gone a few steps before he stopped abruptly and looked at her with a ray of renewed hope.

"It's just now come to me! I think I know where she might be," he said in a rush. "Let's go!"

He urged Angela down the road and the two of them began jogging toward the group of barns that made up the working area of the ranch yard. By the time they reached the collection of buildings and connecting cattle pens, they could see several cowboys with flashlights searching the grounds.

The scene was surreal and Angela kept thinking at any moment she would wake up and find Melanie asleep and safe in her little bed. But the urgent tug of Jubal's hand on hers was a reminder that this was no nightmare and the outcome could be even worse.

"Where—are—we going, Jubal?" she asked between gasps for air. Already they'd run a long distance from the house. The exertion, coupled with fear for her daughter's safety, had left her legs on the verge of collapsing, but she staggered after him, unwilling to give in and rest for even a few precious seconds.

"The horse barn. Remember how infatuated she was that day you brought her to see the new baby?" he reminded her. "Maybe she got tired of walking and decided to make a detour."

Angela wiped her tangled hair out of her eyes as they rounded a metal gate and hurried across a dusty lot. A few feet away, in a nearby pen, she could hear cattle lowing and she prayed that Melanie had not scooted under the fence and walked among the herd. Most of them were docile creatures, but they could inadvertently trample or kick her.

"Yes. And she—wants that pony—for Christmas," Angela added, then prayed aloud, "Oh God—let her be in there!"

Since both of their flashlights had gone dead during their run, Angela was relieved to see dim night lights burning over each horse's stall inside the barn, illuminating the alleyway that ran the full length of the cavernous building.

"Melanie! Melanie, are you in here?" Jubal called.

The sound of his voice echoed through the building, but all they could hear in reply was a low nicker, the shuffling of hooves among wood shavings and the creak of the wind as it skimmed across the metal roof far above their heads.

"You take that side," Jubal said, pointing to the left. "I'll take the right and we'll meet at the foaling area. She might have gone there thinking the baby horse would still be there."

Nodding, Angela hurried away from him and quickly began to inspect each stall. Across from her, Jubal did the same.

By the time she neared the end of the long row with no sign of Melanie, her spirits began to plummet. She'd thought Jubal's idea of the horse barn had been a good one. But who knew what went through a child's mind? Like Matt said, she could have headed toward his house to see Jess. In any case, she was lost in the dark, on a ranch that stretched for thousands and thousands of acres.

Her mind was leaping to all sorts of horrendous scenarios when Jubal suddenly called out.

"Over here, Angie!"

Stumbling across the wide alleyway, she raced toward the sound of his voice and found him inside the next to the last stall. A paint horse was standing quietly to one side, his tail switching, his ears perked toward the man that had entered his domain. As for Jubal, he was in the corner, kneeling over something that was presently obscured from Angela's sight. The idea that it was Melanie caused Angela's breath to catch in horror.

"Jubal! Jubal, is it Melanie?"

Glancing over his shoulder, he lifted his hand and silently motioned for her to join him.

Angela forced her spongy legs to move forward until

she was standing close enough to peer over his shoulder. What she saw then caused her to break into great sobs of relief. Melanie was curled up in a pile of soft wood shavings, sound asleep.

"She's asleep. And it doesn't look like a hair on her head has been harmed," he said quietly.

"The horse—he could have stomped her to death!" Angela exclaimed with dismay. "Instead he's standing here as if he's guarding her!"

Looking up at her, Jubal smiled knowingly. "Of course he's guarding her. He knows she's a child and has to be watched over."

Angela closed her eyes as tears of relief rolled down her face. "Angels around the tree," she murmured wondrously, then falling to her knees, she leaned forward and kissed Jubal's cheek. "I think I'm finally beginning to believe in miracles."

He looked at her then, and hope fluttered in her heart like a bird just learning to fly. There was love shining in his eyes, the promise that nothing and no one would ever tear them apart again.

Briefly, he tenderly cupped the side of her face with his hand, then turned to Melanie and lifted her into his arms.

As he cradled the child against his chest, she stirred and gazed sleepily up at him.

"Are you my daddy?" she mumbled tiredly.

Bending his head, he placed his cheek against his daughter's. "Yes, my little darling. I am your daddy. For always."

Hours later, after everyone on the ranch had been alerted that Melanie had been found and the happy ending had been told and retold, Angela lay in Jubal's arms, her head resting on his shoulder as she gazed out the window at the winter stars.

As soon as the commotion of the search for Melanie had ended and Nicci had examined the child to make sure nothing was wrong, Jubal had driven the three of them to his house. By then, their daughter was wide-awake and had spent close to an hour recounting her adventure to her father, until she'd fallen asleep in his arms.

He'd carried her to bed and now she was safely asleep in the bedroom next to theirs, no doubt dreaming of Christmas and her pony. As for Angela, she was still marveling over all that had happened and the fact that Jubal had just made love to her in a way that said he'd never let her go.

"Jubal," she said quietly. "I think it's about time I told you something."

With a good-natured groan, he turned his head toward her and nestled his face in the curve of her shoulder. "Don't tell me you want to have another 'talk' like the last one. I don't think I could live through it."

Smiling in the darkness, she twisted toward him and rested her hand against the side of his face. "Well," she drawled. "I actually do have another confession. But it's not nearly as shocking as the last one. And I figure by now it's something you already know. But I want to tell you anyway."

"Hmm. Are you sure now is the time to do all this talking?"

He pressed his lips to the side of her neck and she groaned as goose bumps scattered across her naked skin.

"All I'm going to say is that I love you. I don't think I ever stopped loving you—even after you married Evette."

The seriousness of her words had him propping his head in his hand as he gazed down at her. "I didn't know—

when I first saw you on the ranch, you acted as though you hated me."

"I hated that you'd left me—that you never attempted to find me—but I never hated you. I tried, but I couldn't."

His free hand lifted and stroked her cheek. "Even after the ordeal with Evette, I couldn't forget you. I tried to date again, but other women didn't interest me. So I threw myself into my work and tried to convince myself that I was happy. But I didn't know what happy was until now," he confessed.

Bittersweet emotions flooded her heart and spilled through her chest. "You can forgive me for not telling you about Melanie?"

"Darling, darling," he whispered on a groan, "earlier this evening, I had already decided that somehow I had to make things work for us. Then when you called and said that Melanie was missing—it jolted everything into perspective. Nothing about the past matters anymore. We've forgiven each other. I love you and Melanie—love you like crazy." He rubbed his cheek against the top of her head. "Before the new year rolls around, we're going to be married. And you know what else I think? My parents need to meet their granddaughter."

Surprised, she eased her head back to look at him. "Your parents? They might not be too pleased to learn you have a child with me."

He rubbed the back of his fingers against her cheek. "I have a feeling they won't be able to resist Melanie—or you, for that matter."

She turned her head enough to kiss the palm of his hand. "I hope you're right."

He eased her head back down to his shoulder. "Mom

and Dad couldn't understand that love and honesty were all I wanted in a marriage. But they'll learn. When you've been blessed with a second chance as you and I have been, Angie, it's easy to forgive and accept. Don't you think it's about time you visited your parents, too?"

Before tonight, Angela would have completely rejected that idea. After all, they'd disowned her as though she'd been a farm hand to hire or fire at their own discretion. But Jubal was right. The two of them had so much. A daughter and each other. They had love.

And it would be nice, she thought, to show Oscar and Nadine that Jubal was her husband, that they had a daughter and would eventually have more children together.

Yes, forgiveness was a very special thing. Almost as special as the man lying next to her.

"Yes, I think it would be good for them to meet my family," she softly agreed. "Good for all of us."

A year later, the big house on the Sandbur Ranch was ablaze with Christmas lights and vibrating with the sounds of music and laughter. The evening was particularly warm for Christmas Eve and the front doors to the house had been thrown open. Guests had spilled onto the long porch, many of them dancing on the concrete floor.

Angela and Jubal were one of the couples who'd sought the cooler outside air and were presently wrapped in each other's arms as they moved slowly to a countrified rendition of "White Christmas." Beneath Angela's red velvet dress was the very visible evidence of her pregnancy.

"Have I told you how gorgeous you look tonight?" Jubal murmured near her ear.

"Oh, this is about the tenth time, but I'm not complaining," she said, her smile radiating pure happiness.

He glanced down at the V of her neckline, but instead of the tempting sight of cleavage, he focused on the little horse pinned above her left breast.

"I've bought you all sorts of nice jewelery since we've been married, but you chose to wear this piece tonight. I'll never understand women."

She chuckled softly. "That's because it's special to me. You gave it to me at a time when I didn't have much hope—at least, not for the two of us. And I didn't even know the horse was made from real gemstones until a lot later when Juliet told me."

He pressed a tiny kiss to the tip of her ear. "Everything I've ever given you is real, my darling. Especially my love."

Their first anniversary was less than five days away. Angela could hardly believe that so much time had already spun by. So much had happened in their lives during the past year. So many good things. She'd sailed through each day on a happy cloud.

In the past few months, she and Jubal had actually begun to build decent relationships with their parents, and she'd finished the last courses she'd needed to get her teaching degree. Soon she would be taking the state exam to acquire her teacher's certificate. However, Angela didn't have plans to go to work anytime soon. With the baby coming, she wanted to devote her time to being a mother and wife. There would be plenty of time in the future for her to devote herself to a classroom full of children.

"Hmm. What a difference a year makes," she murmured. "This time last year, I was working in the kitchen with Cook and dancing in a pair of nasty jeans. Now I'm dressed in velvet and diamonds."

Jubal grunted. "I could have killed Lex that night when I spotted you in his arms."

"Jubal!" she gently scolded. "I love Lex. As a brother, that is."

He chuckled. "Yeah, so do I. Did I ever tell you that I thanked him for dancing with you that night?"

Bemused, she glanced up at him. "No. Why did you do that?"

He grinned down at her. "Seeing you with him shook me up. Reminded me of everything I was about to lose."

Chuckling, she patted her bulging stomach. "Well, that obviously didn't happen," she said. Her expression turned winsome. "You know, as happy as I am tonight, I still feel a tad guilty to think of Cook working so hard to put on this shindig and me not back there helping her."

Jubal shook his head at her. "She doesn't want you back there with her. She wants you to be enjoying yourself with your husband. Besides, she has a new girl to help her."

Angela nodded thoughtfully. "Yeah. And from what Mercedes says, she desperately needed the job. She has a young son to raise and no husband to help."

"Don't worry. Cook will draw the woman under her caring wing."

The music suddenly ended and Jubal led Angela over to a wicker couch and helped her into it. As he took a seat beside her, they both turned to look at a second group of guests filtering out the door. Among them were Geraldine and her longtime beau.

"Geraldine seems especially happy tonight," Jubal commented. "Guess she's looking forward to Christmas."

Angela smiled knowingly. "Why wouldn't she be glowing? She has Senator Wolfe Maddson with her tonight. Cook and I are both wagering they'll get married soon. Doesn't he look dashing?"

Jubal glanced down the long porch to where a tall, muscular man with iron gray hair was whispering something in Geraldine's ear.

"Well, I suppose from a woman's view, the man could be called dashing," he conceded.

"Geraldine has something else to be happy about," Angela added. "She's just gotten word that Mercedes and Gabe are expecting their first child this coming spring. Looks like our little one will have a playmate his own age."

Jubal chuckled. "Yeah, the population on the Sandbur is definitely growing. And speaking of children, I wonder how our daughter is enjoying the kids' party that's going on upstairs?"

"I'm sure she's having a ball. Jess is talking up a storm now, so she's probably giving him all kinds of orders." She closed her hand around Jubal's. "I'm just wondering how you're going to top the gift she got for Christmas last year. I'll never forget the look on her face when she walked outside and saw the paint pony on the lawn."

"Yeah," Jubal grunted with amusement. "She looked pretty smug. Just like she knew Santa was going to come through for her all along."

Smiling, Angela looked curiously up at him. "So now that she has King, what is Santa bringing our daughter this year?"

Jubal patted her tummy. "A little brother."

"Besides that."

"Oh, don't worry," he said impishly. "It will be enough to make her happy without making her too spoiled."

"I hope you're right."

Grinning wryly, he leaned closer and tapped a finger against her nose. "You haven't quit believing in miracles, have you, Mrs. Jamison?"

Laughing softly, she gently cupped her hand against the side of his face. "How could I, darling? I'm living one every day of my life."

* * * * *

Don't miss Lex's story
coming in January 2009!

Here is a sneak preview of
A STONE CREEK CHRISTMAS,
the latest in Linda Lael Miller's acclaimed
McKETTRICK *series.*

A lonely horse brought vet Olivia O'Ballivan to Tanner Quinn's farm, but it's the rancher's love that might cause her to stay.

A STONE CREEK CHRISTMAS
Available December 2008
from Silhouette Special Edition

Tanner heard the rig roll in around sunset. Smiling, he wandered to the window. Watched as Olivia O'Ballivan climbed out of her Suburban, flung one defiant glance toward the house and started for the barn, the golden retriever trotting along behind her.

Taking his coat and hat down from the peg next to the back door, he put them on and went outside. He was used to being alone, even liked it, but keeping company with Doc O'Ballivan, bristly though she sometimes was, would provide a welcome diversion.

He gave her time to reach the horse Butterpie's stall, then walked into the barn.

The golden retriever came to greet him, all wagging tail and melting brown eyes, and he bent to stroke her soft, sturdy back. "Hey, there, dog," he said.

Sure enough, Olivia was in the stall, brushing Butterpie down and talking to her in a soft, soothing voice that touched something private inside Tanner and made him want to turn on one heel and beat it back to the house.

He'd be damned if he'd do it, though.

This was *his* ranch, *his* barn. Well-intentioned as she was, *Olivia* was the trespasser here, not him.

"She's still very upset," Olivia told him, without turning to look at him or slowing down with the brush.

Shiloh, always an easy horse to get along with, stood contentedly in his own stall, munching away on the feed Tanner had given him earlier. Butterpie, he noted, hadn't touched her supper as far as he could tell.

"Do you know anything at all about horses, Mr. Quinn?" Olivia asked.

He leaned against the stall door, the way he had the day before, and grinned. He'd practically been raised on horseback; he and Tessa had grown up on their grandmother's farm in the Texas hill country, after their folks divorced and went their separate ways, both of them too busy to bother with a couple of kids. "A few things," he said. "And I mean to call you Olivia, so you might as well return the favor and address me by my first name."

He watched as she took that in, dealt with it, decided on an approach. He'd have to wait and see what that turned out to be, but he didn't mind. It was a pleasure just watching Olivia O'Ballivan grooming a horse.

"All right, *Tanner*," she said. "This barn is a disgrace. When are you going to have the roof fixed? If it snows again, the hay will get wet and probably mold..."

He chuckled, shifted a little. He'd have a crew out there the following Monday morning to replace the roof and shore up the walls—he'd made the arrangements over a week before—but he felt no particular compunction to explain that. He was enjoying her ire too much; it made her color rise and her hair fly when she turned her head, and the faster breathing made her perfect breasts go up and down in an enticing rhythm. "What makes you so sure I'm a greenhorn?" he asked mildly, still leaning on the gate.

At last she looked straight at him, but she didn't move from Butterpie's side. "Your hat, your boots—that fancy red truck you drive. I'll bet it's customized."

Tanner grinned. Adjusted his hat. "Are you telling me real cowboys don't drive red trucks?"

"There are lots of trucks around here," she said. "Some of them are red, and some of them are new. And *all* of them are splattered with mud or manure or both."

"Maybe I ought to put in a car wash, then," he teased. "Sounds like there's a market for one. Might be a good investment."

She softened, though not significantly, and spared him a cautious half smile, full of questions she probably wouldn't ask. "There's a good car wash in Indian Rock," she informed him. "People go there. It's only forty miles."

"Oh," he said with just a hint of mockery. "*Only* forty miles. Well, then. Guess I'd better dirty up my truck if I want to be taken seriously in these here parts. Scuff up my boots a bit, too, and maybe stomp on my hat a couple of times."

Her cheeks went a fetching shade of pink. "You are twisting what I said," she told him, brushing Butterpie again, her touch gentle but sure. "I meant…"

Tanner envied that little horse. Wished he had a furry hide, so he'd need brushing, too.

"You *meant* that I'm not a real cowboy," he said. "And you could be right. I've spent a lot of time on construction sites over the last few years, or in meetings where a hat and boots wouldn't be appropriate. Instead of digging out my old gear, once I decided to take this job, I just bought new."

"I bet you don't even *have* any old gear," she challenged, but she was smiling, albeit cautiously, as though she might withdraw into a disapproving frown at any second.

He took off his hat, extended it to her. "Here," he teased. "Rub that around in the muck until it suits you."

She laughed, and the sound—well, it caused a powerful and wholly unexpected shift inside him. Scared the hell out of him and, paradoxically, made him yearn to hear it again.

* * * * *

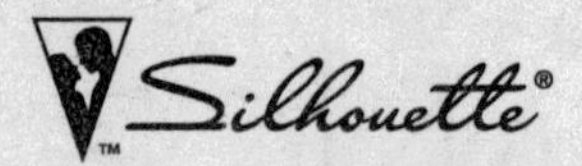

SPECIAL EDITION®

COMING NEXT MONTH

#1945 THE STRANGER AND TESSA JONES—
Christine Rimmer
Bravo Family Ties
The Bravos meet the Jones Gang as two of Christine Rimmer's famous Special Edition families come together in one very special book. Snowed in with an amnesiac stranger during a freak blizzard, Tessa Jones soon finds out her guest is none other than heartbreaker Ash Bravo. And that's when things really heat up....

#1946 PLAIN JANE AND THE PLAYBOY—Marie Ferrarella
Fortunes of Texas: Return to Red Rock
To kill time at a New Year's party, playboy Jorge Mendoza shows the host's teenage son how to woo the ladies. The random target of Jorge's charms: wallflower Jane Gilliam. But with one kiss at midnight, introverted Jane turns the tables on this would-be Casanova, as the commitment-phobe falls for her hook, line and sinker!

#1947 COWBOY TO THE RESCUE—Stella Bagwell
Men of the West
Hired to investigate the mysterious death of the Sandbur Ranch matriarch's late husband, private investigator Christina Logan enlists the help of cowboy-to-the-core Lex Saddler, Sandbur's youngest—and singlest—scion. Together, they find the truth...and each other.

#1948 REINING IN THE RANCHER—Karen Templeton
Wed in the West
Horse breeder Johnny Griego is blindsided by the news—both his ex-girlfriend Thea Benedict *and* his teenage daughter are pregnant. Never one to shirk responsibility, Johnny does the right thing and proposes to Thea. But Thea wants happily-ever-after, not a mere marriage of convenience. Can she rein in the rancher enough to have both?

#1949 SINGLE MOM SEEKS...—Teresa Hill
All newly divorced Lily Tanner wants is a safe, happy life with her two adorable daughters. Until hunky FBI agent Nick Malone moves in next door with his orphaned nephew. Now the pretty single mom's single days just might be numbered....

#1950 I STILL DO—Christie Ridgway
During a chance reunion in Vegas, former childhood sweethearts Will Dailey and Emily Garner let loose a little and make good on an old pledge—to wed each other if they weren't otherwise taken by age thirty! But in the cold light of day, the firefighter and librarian's quickie marriage doesn't seem like such a bright idea. Would their whim last a lifetime?

SSECNM1208BPA